Nathanial Thatcher

The Hyperion Secret

I0600936

Nathanial Thatcher

The Hyperion Secret

T. C. Chappell

Blue DOT Books

"*THE QUICKEST WAY IS SOMETIMES THE LONGEST.*"

-NEIL GAIMAN

CONTENTS

Nathanial Thatcher

The Hyperion Secret

Chapter One

NATHANIAL'S ITCHY AWAKENING

athanial Thatcher sat sandwiched between two of his buddies on a picnic table in the recess yard of his middle school. His unruly dirty blonde hair flopped over his brown eyes, which gave him excuse enough to suavely throw his head back on several occasions. It was lucky he didn't bonk heads with the two beside him, as they too seemed to have the same crippling fear of hairdressers. They simultaneously swished their bangs back as if they were a part of a poorly rehearsed dance team.

In fact, there was nothing about Nathanial that would lead anyone to believe he was different from any other boy. By his looks, one would guess that he was perfectly healthy, happy, and getting to be a little handsome. How could anyone tell that he'd been a prisoner just a year before? Not a hardened criminal who glares out mischievously from behind cold steel bars, but the wrongfully accused who pines for the freedom he deserves. In Nathanial's case, his weak immune system had been the jailer who had kept him locked away in his sterilized bedroom most of his life; that was until a year ago, when, on his twelfth birthday, his life was changed forever.

Nathanial didn't know how he'd earned his freedom, but after twelve years of uncontrollable coughing fits, with his only human contact being his mother and his doctor, and having read more books than a fifty-year-old scholar, he honestly didn't care why he was suddenly fit as a fiddle. He just wanted to start experiencing the world he'd only read about. He was so grateful, he didn't even complain about the annoying itchiness in his ears, even if it had been getting progressively worse each day.

Nathanial pretended he was pushing back some of his long curls as he scratched the tips of his ears.

"So, Nathan, you thought about what I said about your birthday or what?" Jason asked as he punched Nathanial's arm.

"Yeah, I thought about it," Nathanial said without enthusiasm. "It's just, my mom really wants to have it at our place. This being the first time I can actually have a party, and all."

"But dude," Brad protested from his right, surrounding him with peer pressure. "This is the big *one three*! You're going to be in the teens now.

You have to *really* party. Not have a momma's party! Jason's parents are going to be outta town a whole week this time. You gotta have the party at his place."

"For real," Jason pushed, "Brad knows what he's talking about. He's been to all my non-parental parties. I got the whole thing worked out. I even invited Stacy."

Both Jason and Brad broke out into huge grins and turned their gazes from Nathanial's reddening face to a group of girls across the yard chatting on a swing set. Nathanial quickly looked away from the cute, preppy, dark-haired girl who garnered most of the attention in the middle of the pack and pushed his hair past his itchy ears again.

"I don't know why you think that would convince me. I don't even talk to Stacy," Nathanial said, shrugging to show nonchalance but feeling a twist in his stomach at the prospect of getting to know the cutest girl in class.

Jason snorted. "Exactly. But don't pretend you don't want to. This would be the perfect opportunity."

"Yeah," Brad said getting excited. "We can play truth or dare—and I'll dare her to kiss you!"

"Shut up," Nathanial said, pushing him away.

Brad high-fived Jason.

Just then, Nathanial caught someone looking at him from the other side of the schoolyard's chain-link fence. She didn't appear to be much older than him, but there was a strange maturity in the confidence of her stance and the shine in her eyes. Her hair was dark and sticking up in all directions in a wild-girl kind of way. Her skin was bronze and shiny. Her eyes were sharp and bright orange, like a cat's. Nathanial felt she was familiar, and the lack of recollection pulled heavy on his mind.

"Hey!" Jason yelled and gave Nathanial a shove.

Nathanial broke his stare and turned angrily to Jason. "What?"

"Did you not hear a word I just said?"

Nathanial shook his head and looked back toward the chain-link fence. Jason followed his gaze. There was no one there.

"What is up with you?" Jason asked.

The school bell rang. As everyone headed inside, Nathanial scanned the yard for any sign of the wild girl.

"Come on, man," Brad said dragging Nathanial into the pack by his shirtsleeve.

As Nathanial fell into the routine of his day, what had seemed like an important sighting in the schoolyard soon had less substance than a daydream.

It took another week of peer pressure, but Nathanial gave in and it was time for the non-parental birthday party. He had always wanted to have a real birthday party, so why was he so nervous about it now? Maybe it was just that he didn't know what to expect. His past birthdays had consisted of monitoring his coughing fits and only being let out of his sanitized room for an hour if his coughing hadn't been bad the days before. It had been just him and his mom and a birthday cake, and it was the hour he had most looked forward to every year. How many times had he imagined having a party full of friends to play games with and a pile of presents to open? Now it seemed he didn't know what to do at a real birthday party. Was he really going to have to play truth or dare? Maybe he wasn't the party kind of guy after all. Having only just started his second year at school, he wondered if after all his pining for social interaction, now that he'd experienced it, maybe it wasn't for him.

He hadn't been expecting so much attention last year when he started school for the first time ever. He'd made friends easily, but soon realized it was more like his friends chose him rather than he chose them, and he didn't like the way he was always being pressured into things by Jason and

Brad. Maybe he shouldn't even go to the party after all. That would probably be for the best.

"Ok sweetie, we're here," said Nathanial's mom, Suzy, as she parked the car at the curb in front of a nicely renovated colonial home.

"Huh?" Nathanial said, pulling himself from his thoughts. "Oh, yeah. Cool."

"You ok, Nathanial?" Suzy asked, brushing his hair back out of his face.

"Yeah, Mom. I'm fine." He gave her a falsely confident smile.

"Don't be nervous, honey," she said, starting to look worried. "This is what you wanted wasn't it?"

"Of course," he said with a crack in his voice. "Well, better not be late for my own party."

Nathanial got out of the car and slowly walked up the brick path toward the house, his hands in his jeans pockets. He stopped to look back at his mom and tugged at the collar of his brand-new button-up shirt. She watched him while she nervously bit her nails.

He waved and mouthed, "I'm ok," and waited for her to pull away before moving any further. He was about to reach the porch steps when he thought he saw the wild girl's reflection scattered within the floral pattern of the glass front door. He quickly turned, but only the rustle of rose bushes awaited his curious stare.

The front door swung open and Jason appeared with his hands held high saying, "The man of the hour has arrived! Come on, bro. You are about to have a party you'll never forget!"

Jason led Nathanial through the large chandelier covered entryway and into a dining room with balloons, party favors, and a grand pile of colorful presents stacked upon a glass dining table. Nathanial was surprised by the amount of people drinking sodas and listening to music in high-backed chairs around the table or chilling in the cushioned armchairs in the corners of the room. Many of these kids weren't exactly what he'd call friends, as everyone tended to socialize in smaller groups, but all of them were high enough on the preppy social ladder to be cordial with Jason and anyone who was a part of his clique. They all applauded Nathanial's entrance and cheered, "Happy birthday!"

"Wow," Nathanial said, taken aback by the amount of effort that had gone into the event. Jason wasn't known for his altruism, and Nathanial expected the extravagance was more his showing off than generosity. "You really went all out."

He scanned the dozen or so faces, but didn't see Stacy. Maybe it had been just another one of Jason's pranks at his expense, telling him he'd invited her. Or maybe she was invited and didn't want to come. Nathanial's nerves played tug-of-war: on one side, disappointment at her absence; on the other, pure relief. He wouldn't be put in a position to make a fool out of himself if she wasn't there.

Jason caught Nathanial searching the room. He hit him on his back and said, "Wait for it." He pulled out his iPhone and changed the music to a hip-hop version of "Happy Birthday." Stacy entered the room wearing the cutest flower-patterned summer dress. She was carrying a birthday cake in with thirteen lit candles on it.

Jason laughed when he saw Nathanial's jaw drop and his cheeks flush.

Stacy put the birthday cake down on the table and said, "Happy birthday, Nathanial."

"Thanks, Stacy," Nathanial said, hating the heat he felt on his face.

Everyone started to chant, "Blow them out, blow them out, blow them out!"

Nathanial's instinct was to concentrate on the wish he made every birthday—*I wish I was well*—but he caught himself. He leaned over the table and blew out all thirteen candles in one big huff, not even bothering to make a wish. He was well, and there was nothing more he could wish for. He let the moment sink in, brushed away the butterflies of awkward social interactions, and took in his deep appreciation for his health, freedom, and new life opportunities. Everyone cheered.

"Cut the cake and let's get on with the celebrations!" Jason yelled holding up a knife.

Over the next couple of hours, there were some video games played, a little time spent in the pool, and a serious game of ping-pong, in which Stacy kicked his butt. Nathanial started to feel comfortable around the crowd, and even with Stacy, as they settled down in the living room to watch a movie on the biggest flat-screen TV he'd ever seen. Then Brad had to go and open his mouth.

"It's time we liven things up here, don't you think, people?" Brad yelled to the group gathered on the sofas.

"Oh, here we go, let me guess…" a girl sitting in a beanbag chair said, rolling her eyes at Brad. "Could you be suggesting we play truth or dare again?"

"Why, Lisa? You too chicken?" Brad said.

"It's not me that's chicken, *Brad*. We all know you just want to make people kiss, but then when it's your turn, you always pick *truth*, so, who's the real chicken?"

Everyone laughed.

"So, do you have a better idea?" Brad challenged Lisa.

"Let's just cut to the chase and play seven minutes in heaven. There are three closets in here, so we can have three couples at a time, a pair in each. We'll blindfold three boys and put them with three blindfolded girls in the closets. Whatever happens, happens!"

Brad's eyes were wide and his mouth slightly open.

"What? Is that too lively for you?" Lisa said with a satisfied smirk at his expression.

Brad scoffed and said, "No. Let's do it."

Nathanial was terrified. He glanced over to Stacy and horrifyingly she looked over to him just after. He quickly darted his eyes away. She must have thought he was staring at her. She probably thought he wanted a closet with her. What was he going to do? There must be a good excuse to leave.... Could he say his mother would be worried if he wasn't home soon? Nathanial looked at the clock on the wall. She wasn't supposed to pick him up for another couple of hours. He couldn't use the mom excuse anyway. That would be lame.

"Well, obviously the birthday boy should be one of the guys to go first," Jason said. "And so should you, Brad, for getting us all into this mess."

Most the group laughed and agreed.

Nathanial's brain went numb. Someone tied a bandanna around his eyes and he was shoved into a closet. Someone else was pushed into him amidst the clothes. Then the door was shut. He could only hear muffled laughter from the other side of the door and the quickened breaths of the girl beside him.

"Hello?" Nathanial said timidly.

There was no answer.

"Um," Nathanial tried again. "We don't have to do anything. This is a stupid game."

There was still no word from his partner in the dark. Nathanial's ears were really starting to itch now. He thought there was no harm in scratching them since no one could see.

"We aren't supposed to talk," the girl's voice finally whispered.

Nathanial stopped scratching his ears. He was pretty sure that it was Stacy.

"But you're right," she said softly. "It is a stupid game."

It was definitely Stacy, and was that disappointment in her voice? Did she *want* to kiss him? Should he make a move? Was he ready for that? Would it hurt her feelings if he didn't? He knew just about everyone in his class had already kissed someone, but he barely knew this girl and he wasn't sure how he felt about her. She was pretty and popular, but it hadn't been those things that had drawn his attention to her. It was more like a feeling of familiarity. Since he first caught her dark eyes from across the classroom, she had always reminded him of someone else. He could never figure out who it was. For some reason, he had expected her to have an accent.

Nathanial felt fingers run through his hair and his heart skipped a beat. She smelled of flowers. He could feel her coming even closer to him. She moved her fingertips over the bandanna right where it rested on his ears. It drove him crazy. He really wanted to scratch! Then she pulled off the bandanna. He could see her outline from the light coming through the cracks around the door. She already had taken her blindfold off and he could see a smile from the light hitting her cheek.

Then her fingers went over his right ear again, and, for the first time in months, the itching stopped. But instead of relief, he felt anxiety. Stacy stopped moving. Her smile fell into a frown. Her hand closed on the tip of Nathanial's ear.

"What is it?" Nathanial asked.

Stacy stepped back. Nathanial reached up and felt his own ears. There was definitely something wrong there.

Stacy backed into the door and opened it with her hand behind her back. She watched the light fall onto Nathanial as it poured in over him. Then she continued to back away.

"Whoa there, Stacy, your time ain't up!" Jason said, laughing at her exit. "Jeez, Nate. You that bad a kisser?"

Nathanial slowly walked out into the room filled with half a dozen giggling eighth graders. He needed to get out of there before any of them noticed. He only hoped Stacy would have the grace not to say anything. From the look of her, she was too freaked out to anyhow.

Jason looked back and forth between Stacy and Nathanial trying to figure out the reason for the extreme awkwardness. Nathanial knew he had about point-two seconds to get out of there before Jason followed Stacy's stare right to his ears. He was only thankful he had let his hair grow enough for a little cover.

"Sorry, guys. I gotta get home," he said darting toward the entryway.

He didn't get three steps before Jason grabbed his arm and swung him around.

"Dude," he said pushing back Nathanial's hair. "What is this? Since when are you a Vulcan? Is this for real?"

Jason pulled on Nathanial's ear. Nathanial slapped Jason's arm away and turned to run for the door only to quickly stop in his tracks. His path was blocked: It was the wild girl standing proud as a peacock with her hands on her hips and a smile on her face.

"Hello Nate-a-roonie!" she said enthusiastically.

"Wha…" Nathanial gawked. "Do I know you?"

"'Course you do!" she said, grabbing him by the arm and pulling him into a hug.

Nathanial didn't know quite what to think of this and was waiting for Jason to start having a fit behind him. When the wild girl let go, Nathanial slowly turned back to face the group, wondering why they were so quiet.

"Jason?" Nathanial took a step toward him, but Jason did not so much as blink. "What did you do?" Nathanial asked looking back at the wild girl.

She chuckled and put an arm around him. "I didn't do anything. In fact, that's why I've shown up. We wanted to get to you a lot sooner, but there's been some trouble since last I saw you. I was only allowed to show myself to you again if you made any signs of actually turning and well…" she held her arm out toward the frozen group, "I think this is as good a sign as any."

"Are you saying *I* did this?" Nathanial exclaimed.

"Yep! Quite the forget-trick you're playing on them. When they wake up, they'll be wondering what they were even doing in this room. We sprites use this one a lot when we're borrowing something they've come to get. Gives us a chance to replace it before they've noticed its absence. We better go, though. It doesn't hold for long."

The girl pulled Nathanial through the entryway and out the door. She finally let go of him when they were outside on the sidewalk.

"Who are you?" Nathanial asked.

She tilted her fluffy head and said, "Oh, yeah. I keep forgetting. I'm Bunny! We've met before. I'm sure once we get you back through a Niche, you'll start remembering."

"Bunny? A Niche?" Nathanial asked slowly. Was this girl for real? He followed uncertainly; he was intrigued. From her first appearance, he had felt anxiety that he was forgetting something important, but he couldn't understand how she and this feeling were related.

"Yeah, a Niche. It's a door. A little door. Only sprites use them."

"There's that word again. Are you a sprite?" Nathanial jogged to keep up with her quick steps.

"I'm not the only one in present company." She

winked.

Nathanial stopped for a moment and felt his ears. He then ran up beside Bunny and looked at her ears through her puffy hair. They were slightly pointy, too!

He was amazed. "How did this happen?" He then considered the folklore and fairytales he had read and wondered which one of them might suddenly be of real use. "Are sprites like fairies or elves, or what exactly?"

"Eh," Bunny said with a crinkle of her nose. "Faery is a broad term. It encompasses lots of different subspecies that are in tune with nature. But like with most of life, time changed us, branching us off from one another. Some species thrived, while others dwindled. We're really the only ones left that can rival humanity in population. Maybe it was because of our success that the others faded. Humans used to be a part of faery, too, believe it or not." She stopped and darted through some bushes. "Here we go."

"Bunny?" he whispered in surprise at how suddenly she'd vanished into the shrubbery.

She stepped back out from behind a tree, startling Nathanial.

"Let's take a shortcut," she said and waved him to follow her.

Bunny took a pouch from her belt, opened it, and held it out to Nathanial.

"What's this?" he asked taking it and looking into the bag at the sparkling substance it held.

"It's my specialty. I'm a dust sprite. Most sprites stay small and live their lives contently amongst their own kind, only visiting the humans for work purposes and never in need of the dust. Then there are a few who like to wander amongst the humans and, for that, they come to me." She nodded to the pouch. "There are some travel tunnels that can do the same thing, but they are few and far between and only go to specific destinations." She thought for a second and scratched her nose. "Well, some sprites do use dust for getting even smaller, you know, to get into hard-to-reach places, or they mix it with another kind of dust to make objects fit together that normally wouldn't, but that's not why I make it. My stuff is all nat-ur-al!"

"So...what am I supposed to do?" Nathanial asked.

"You're gonna put it on! It can shrink you or stretch you, depending on your natural state. If you're big, it will make you small; if you're small, it will make you big. Wanting to be bigger when you're big or smaller when you're small requires some manipulation of the dust. But we need you small right now. It's the only way to go through the Niche."

Nathanial looked around the woods. "Niche, like a door. There's a door around here?"

"A Niche, yes."

"How do you know?"

"Good question," she said looking around. "It's really Boss who should be teaching you this stuff, but I guess you'll have plenty of him soon enough. Ok, so, in every corner there's a Niche, right? Most of them are quick auto escapes in case a sprite needs a fast exit, only one direction, in. But then there are corners that are more desirable. Better locations, better builds. The really good ones have a travel flow in both directions. You can go in and out and be connected to the same place reliably. The weak one-ways usually just lead to the largest sprite town around. The ones in these woods here are pretty weak; they will all route one way, but it's the way we're going, so that's ok. If you want to find a Niche, just look for the seams in a corner. This one here is made from two trees that have grown together to form a corner. Do you see it?"

Nathanial looked down at the twisting roots and saw the spot she was describing. "Yeah..." he responded uncertainly.

"Do you see the seams?"

Nathanial squinted. "No."

"You can see them better when you're sprite-sized. Go ahead and use the dust."

Nathanial put his hand in the pouch and grasped some of the sandy substance. He palmed it out in front of him and looked to Bunny for further instructions.

"Just throw it on," Bunny said with a slight giggle.

Nathanial closed his eyes and threw the dust at himself. He felt a tingle in his nose that spread quickly throughout his body. He let out one large uncontrollable sneeze that shot him down to an inch in height within the blink of an eye. He stumbled onto his knees from a disorienting lack of balance. Nathanial took a confused look around, then screamed at the Godzilla-sized Bunny in front of him. Within a moment, she was down to his size and helping him to his feet.

"Now, look at the tree again," Bunny said.

Nathanial felt like he'd just been zapped into the movie *Honey, I Shrunk the Kids*. He faced the skyscraping tree and tried to recall the question Bunny had just asked. It was difficult to concentrate when a new monstrous jungle towered around him, but he forced his attention onto the corner formed by the tree roots. A razor-thin cut formed an indented square where the two roots met.

"I see it!" Nathanial said, amazed. "But where's the doorknob?"

"It's not a door. It's a Niche. Sorry I said it was a door. It's the only thing close to what humans have. Maybe I should have said gate. I'm sure Boss will be better at this. Come on. I'll show you how to get in."

Bunny walked up to the tree and put her hand on the inside of the cut.

"Now, some Niches are guarded. Those are usually for private residences that have been bought by fancy sprites who don't like going through crowded Niche-ways. They'll be marked, telling you not to enter, but most are public and look like this one. Pretty plain right? Factory Niches are marked, too, like yours was, and are often claimed by dust sprites. It's a good place for us to set up shop because factories often lead to the big world of humans—and what better place to sell that which makes you big?"

Nathanial furrowed his brow. "Mine? I have a Niche?"

"Oh, yeah! Boss liked to buy from me there all the time. I always suspected he might be looking for someone from his past. You know, like, someone BIG?" With her hand still buried in the tree she nodded and sent her eyebrows up and down multiple times as if Nathanial should be picking up what she was putting down, but he just stared at her blankly. "Just don't tell him I ever told you that. He can't talk about his past anyway. Like, literally, *he can't*! Anyway, I had other reasons to be by your Niche, too," she looked at him hesitantly. "I just mean I had already invested some time there before I went all dusty," she giggled, and Nathanial knew there was more there than she was saying, which seemed odd for a girl who seemed to say so much. "Oh!" She bounced happily. "There we go!"

The tree bark had molded itself around her hand and she pulled the Niche open.

"Yep, this Niche is free and clear," Bunny continued. "Like most of the Niches in this area, it goes to old headquarters. No one uses them anymore."

As the door swung wide, the bark of the tree let loose of Bunny's hand. They walked into the darkness together and the door shut behind them.

Chapter Two

GOODBYES ARE OVERRATED

*N*athanial didn't know what he had expected to see within the tree trunk Niche, but this wasn't it. All the wood around him seemed milled and processed; boards and planks made the floors and walls. The feel of nature was gone and replaced with that of an eerie ghost town. The lighting within the cavernous enclosure was dim and flickered from many lampposts. The flickering was not due to busted light bulbs or open flame. The light somehow came from the posts themselves, like the luminescent mushrooms Nathanial had read about; many were dying, or already dead.

The wide streets were abandoned. *Out of Business* signs were posted over the shop windows and limp open doors. A huge hamster wheel creaked so loudly it echoed through the streets. It appeared to have once powered an old lift made from a basket and rope. It swung, empty, amidst the towering heights of a compounded apartment building where it had once provided transport for residents going to and from balconies.

Nathanial walked over a littered patch of faded orange posters: *Grit the Gook! Your all-purpose cleaner, all the time!*

"*Grit the Gook*," he whispered to himself. It seemed familiar. "What happened here?" Nathanial asked Bunny.

"Well…" Bunny sighed. "The factory that brought in all the businesses shut down and its headquarters was moved to a wealthier location. With the factory gone, there was no reason for the sprites to stay. When the last sprite decides to leave, this place will dissolve and all the local Niches will be rerouted to the next nearest sprite town. Now that you are about to go, there won't be a reason for me to stay."

"Go?" Nathanial lifted an eyebrow. Bunny nodded and appeared sadly distracted. For the first time since they met they walked on in silence.

For the next few blocks, Nathanial absorbed more of the details within the quiet around him. He marveled at the doors set into the walls several stories above the basket lift that didn't have balconies or stairs, and wondered how they might be reached. He noticed the shops protruding outward were reminiscent of papier-mâché with rough, wrinkled textures and seams that overlapped in multiple colors.

Nathanial wished he could have seen this place in its prime. It must have been quite the sight. Suddenly a twinge of guilt twisted in his gut. Somehow, he felt responsible for the fate that this sprite town had suffered.

At the dead end of the linear town, Bunny finally stopped. They turned toward the corner with a split golden word, *Lyso* on the left and, *torium* on the right. Bunny pushed open the *Lyso-torium* Niche. Light blinded Nathanial momentarily and then he focused out onto his bedroom.

"Wow, you weren't kidding when you said *shortcut*," Nathanial said staring from his tiny perspective into the gigantic space. He looked back and forth from his bedroom to the ghost town. "So this place is inside the walls of my house?"

"Yep." Bunny bounced. "This is a direct Niche. Two-way entry and exit, no need for finagled re-routes within the Niche-way. It's common to have a direct Niche to a large factory, mainly for the workers' sake. Go ahead and use the dust," Bunny said, nodding down to his hand that held the pouch.

Nathanial took out some of the shimmering particles. He closed his eyes, ready to throw it at himself, when Bunny grabbed his hand.

"Oh, wait," she said. "It's a little trickier from here. You're going to need to jump and then *throw* it on."

"What?" Nathanial looked down at what seemed like a fifty-foot drop from the middle of where his bookshelf met his DVD shelf.

"If you do it here, you're just going to squish in the Niche!" Bunny said with a chuckle, but Nathanial didn't find anything funny about that idea.

He swallowed hard, looked again at the drop, and took a step backward. "Maybe you could just lower me down with a rope or something. That might be—AAHHHH," Nathanial screamed. Bunny had pushed him. He fell through the dust he'd been holding, sprung back to his human size, and hit the floor facedown like he'd just rolled out of bed.

Nathanial lay still for another shocked moment until Bunny appeared beside him. She closed the Niche in the shelved corner and then funnily reopened it to peer back through what was now little more than an eyehole.

"Yep, it's official," she said closing the Niche again. "Go through there now and you'll be in Johnsonberry."

Nathanial got to his feet, dusted himself off, and

looked at Bunny with annoyance.

Bunny turned back to Nathanial with a toothy smile and held out a small box.

"Happy birthday," she said with a bounce off her toes.

Nathanial's annoyance faltered and he slowly took the box. "You want to give me a birthday present?"

"I think it just became a tradition. But you're not going to like this one as much as what I gave you last year. This one is more like getting a pair of socks or a hair pick," she said, crinkling her nose.

"You gave me something last year?"

"Yeah, Bossy-Hoss has it."

"Who is this *Boss* guy you keep on about?" Nathanial asked, shaking his head.

"Blahhhh," Bunny said rolling her eyes and dropping her shoulders. "I could just twist the ear points right off that headquarters sprite for what he did to you. You'd better start remembering soon. But now that you've sprung your points, I just know you will!"

Nathanial hurriedly felt his ears again. "Ugh, I almost forgot. By the way Stacy looked at me you'd think I was turning into a werewolf or something. I can never show my face to anyone ever again."

Bunny perked up. "Then maybe you *will* like my

present. It was more so you didn't have to explain anything to your mom but…whatevs!"

Nathanial opened the box. Inside were two flesh-colored half-circle cuffs. He pulled one out and watched it jiggle like gelatin before him.

"Put it on your points," Bunny nodded.

Nathanial crossed to the bathroom and looked into the mirror. He placed the jelly cuff over his pointed ear and watched it mold itself onto the point and squish it down. He put the second one on and watched it do the same.

"That's amazing!" he laughed with relief. "I didn't know what I was going to do by Monday, short of arranging an emergency surgery. This is perfect! Thanks, Bunny!"

"Glad you like them, but you won't have to worry about pointed ears on Monday. Anyways, just keep those until you learn how to shrink the points naturally. I'm not even a pro at it yet, but that's because I'm working on lots of changes at once. I'm prioritizing!"

Nathanial looked over at her uncertainly.

"Eh, you'll see what I mean. Just take it easy for the rest of the evening. Maybe watch a movie with your mom or something. I'm sure she'll be happy you came home early for your birthday." She turned back toward the Niche.

"Wait!" Nathanial called after her. "You're not leaving, are you? I have so many questions!"

Bunny smiled at him. "Sorry, Nate-a-roonie. I'm not your mentor. I just wanted to be the welcome back party, and I'll always check in on you from time to time." She winked and then vanished in glitter.

Nathanial took Bunny's advice and spent the rest of the day with his mom. She had made him his favorite cheesecake and bought him the latest Star Wars movie, which they watched happily. Nathanial kept checking his ears to see if the cuffs were holding and tried not to let it bother him that Bunny insinuated he wouldn't need them on Monday. He contented himself by knowing as long as he had the ear cuffs, he could go on with life as if nothing abnormal had happened.

As he lay in bed that night, his mind wouldn't stop reeling. How could any of it be possible? Was he really a sprite now? Bunny said there were memories missing, like the time he had spent with her and some guy named Boss. And had a sprite done something to take that away? He thought about the posters. *Grit the Gook.* Why was that familiar? *This stuff makes the best Grit the Gook.*

A voice had said that to him once—someone from New York? But he didn't know anyone from outside of town.

Nathanial pictured Stacy and how she had looked at him. Her dark eyes were fearful, but then he realized they were not her eyes at all. They were someone else's—a girl he had cared for and been forced to forget. Her fear was not directed toward him, but instead at a cloaked figure standing aboard a pirate ship in a storm. The cloaked figure pushed Nathanial coldly to the ground. He heard the girl scream.

Nathanial woke up in a sweat. It was morning. He hadn't even realized he had fallen asleep. He sat up to catch his breath and threw off the suffocating covers. He went to the bathroom, filled his hands with cool water from the sink, and dunked his face into his palms. Looking at his reflection, he noticed one of his ear cuffs had fallen off during the night and his stomach flipped to realize that the event of Bunny's appearance hadn't been a part of the realistic nightmare. He jogged back over to his bed and made a mad search for his missing ear cuff. He found it under his pillow, and calmed down after putting it back in place. Then he heard voices from the other room.

Nathanial looked at his clock. It was 9 am on

Sunday. Who was talking to his mom now? He went to his door and put his ear to it. A man's voice vibrated through. Nathanial hesitated to go out in his sky-blue-and-cloud-covered pajamas, but his curiosity took over and he opened the door.

Reaching the end of the hall by tiptoe, Nathanial peered around the corner into the living room. There was a tall man with thick black hair brushed neatly to one side wearing a dark navy suit and tie. He sat at the little nook table across from his mom cupping a drink. He was middle-aged, handsome, and putting on the charm, grinning with perfect teeth and a soft reassuring laugh. Nathanial didn't trust him.

"It's a great opportunity for him, I'm sure you'll agree," the man said.

Suzy looked over some brochures and nodded. "It does sound wonderful, and he's always wanted to travel. It's just..." She sighed and lowered the brochures. "I would miss him so much."

Nathanial furrowed his brows at that. Why would his mom miss him? Who was this guy?

"I know, it is hard to be parted from your son," the man said and put his hand over one of Suzy's, "your only son. But it will be an experience of a lifetime and it's not for long. It'll only be one term to start, and then you can decide together what is best for his future."

"Hey," Nathanial felt it was definitely time to step in, "what's going on in here?"

Both the man and Suzy stood and faced Nathanial. Nathanial took a good stern look at the man's bright-blue eyes and wondered why they appeared so happy to see him.

"Nathanial," Suzy said, "this is Mr. Bozeman from the student exchange program. Your teachers recommended you for placement at an advanced international boarding school. Even your principal called this morning to dote on you. She insists that we listen to Mr. Bozeman's pitch about the program. Apparently, it's a big honor to be selected. You must have really impressed your teachers last year."

"An exchange program?" Nathanial repeated.

Mr. Bozeman stepped forward with a charismatic smile. "Yes. I'll be your mentor for a few months. Along with our private lessons, you'll take some courses with kids from all around the world to learn about each other, the different places each of you come from, and how you can be whatever you want to be if you develop the right tools. It's all about intermingling, internationally, to discover your internal ability to be great."

"You know, you just spouted a lot of fancy

words right then, but it still seems pretty vague for an exchange program. Aren't they supposed to involve swapping one student for another? This doesn't sound like that," Nathanial said, lifting his brow. It was odd for Nathanial to take such a tone with an adult, but the pit of his stomach screamed for him to rebel.

Suzy crossed her arms. She, too, was not used to hearing her son be disrespectful, but Mr. Bozeman just laughed and turned to her to say in a whisper, "Do you mind if I speak with Nathanial alone? I just want him to get to know me one-on-one so he can make a good decision for his future."

Suzy examined Nathanial's tense posture and hesitated, but with another reassuring smile from Mr. Bozeman, she took her leave for the kitchen. Mr. Bozeman gestured Nathanial over. Out of respect for his mother, Nathanial decided to comply.

"Nice pajamas," Mr. Bozeman said poking Nathanial in the stomach.

"Excuse me?" Nathanial turned red.

"Have a seat, kiddo."

Nathanial stood stiff spitefully, but Mr. Bozeman looked him directly in the eye and without a word said, *now.* Nathanial sat down.

"Bunny said you still don't remember a thing,"

Mr. Bozeman said seriously.

Comprehension flooded over Nathanial. "You're one of them!"

Mr. Bozeman looked over his shoulder to see if Suzy heard him. She was cooking pancakes and didn't seem to hear. All the same, Mr. Bozeman said, "Keep your voice down."

"Sorry, I just, I don't know what to think about all this. I was hoping it was a dream, but I still have pointy ears this morning."

"You were hoping it was a dream." Mr. Bozeman laughed. "This was your idea, buddy. Eh, anyway, just tell your mom you'd really like to be a part of the exchange program."

"I don't want to leave my mom," Nathanial protested in a loud whisper.

"You have to. You have no idea the trouble you've caused." Mr. Bozeman's laugh was more annoyed than amused now. "Haven't you always, up until this birthday, made the wish to be well?"

Nathanial's eyes widened and he nodded.

Mr. Bozeman continued, "And you lost three days after a coughing fit on your twelfth birthday."

Nathanial nodded again.

"I'm here to tell you that a wish sprite granted your wish last year—you were with me during those three days. A colleague and I felt it best we take you to have that wish revoked and replaced with another. The first wish stopped you from being our factory and made you a target for the nearest insane asylum. I mean, who wouldn't want to cure a poor boy from seeing the little people that no one else could see, right? Basically, your wish to be well threw a wrench in the gears of all our lives, and when given the opportunity to exchange your wish, you threw a bigger wrench by wishing to become a sprite."

"Why would I do that?"

"Longer story than I can get into at the moment, but just trust me. You need to tell your mom you'll do the program before more than just your ears start to pop out on you."

Suzy came into the room with a plate full of pancakes and sat them down on the table. She considered Nathanial's deer-in-the-headlights stare, then Mr. Bozeman's calm expression.

"Honey," she asked, "everything alright?"

Nathanial took a big gulp, looked to his mother and said, "I'll do it."

When Nathanial said he'd do it he didn't think it meant *now!* But there he stood, an hour later, fully dressed and holding a backpack full of his personal belongings as his mother said a brave goodbye to him without letting her tears get the better of her.

"I can't believe how much you've grown this year," she said with a squeeze of Nathanial's shoulders. "It was a miracle when your immune system finally kicked in. I was so proud when you started school and made friends. You deserve this, baby. I might miss you like crazy, but I'd never stand in your way from this kind of experience. You're going to have so many stories to tell!"

Nathanial just smiled with a nod. His mom understood that he'd pined away, looking out his painted-shut window for more than a decade, dreaming of being a part of the adventures he'd only read about in books or watched in films. Even when the miracle had come and he was free from his room, he had been faced with the reality that before he could see the world, he would have to finish school. So, of course, Suzy was happy for him that his dreams seemed to be coming true sooner than either had thought possible, but the sprite changes he now faced flipped everything on its head. It was all happening fast and the shock was setting in.

Suzy turned to Mr. Bozeman and asked, "Is there a phone number where I can reach Nathanial?"

"All the numbers you'll need are in the brochure," Mr. Bozeman said. "The students don't have direct lines, but they get phone privileges once a week. He can call you and tell you all about the great adventures he's having." Mr. Bozeman smiled reassuringly.

"You will call me then, won't you?" Suzy pleaded to Nathanial.

"'Course mom," he responded as if the question offended him.

She gave Nathanial a huge hug, and he could feel that she had a hard time letting go.

"It was nice meeting you, Suzy Thatcher," Mr. Bozeman said putting his hand out and shaking hers. "We'll take good care of your boy." He put his arm around Nathanial and led him out the door.

Suzy watched from the doorstep as Nathanial got into a dark blue car at the curb. He waved at her from the passenger window. She blew him a kiss and held out her fingers in the *I love you* sign.

Nathanial turned to his driver and apparent mentor and asked, "Now what?"

"Now," Mr. Bozeman said starting up the ignition, "you can call me Boss."

"Boss?" Nathanial snorted. "Why, am I one of your employees now?"

"No, it's a nickname a friend gave me and it stuck."

"So you *are* the one Bunny was telling me about then?"

"I'm sure she mentioned me," Boss said.

"She said you have something of mine that she gave me for my birthday last year."

"I do. We'll get to that," Boss said as he turned another corner.

"Where are we going anyway?" Nathanial said looking around the neighborhood. "You should have taken a left back there for the highway."

Boss turned into a driveway and pushed the clicker attached to his sun visor. A garage door opened in front of them. "We aren't going to the highway. I only borrowed the car for appearance."

Once in the garage, they exited the vehicle and Boss closed the door behind them.

"Ok," Nathanial said looking at the strangers' tools, boxes, and Christmas decorations all around them. "This is weird."

"Come on," Boss said, waving him over. "There's a Niche over here."

"Oh," Nathanial said, and joined Boss by the corner.

"Bunny said she gave you some dust."

Nathanial nodded and pulled the pouch from

his backpack. He threw a handful into the air and both he and Boss shrank in an instant.

Nathanial stood in his tiny form for a second and said, "Hey, I didn't sneeze that time."

"And you stayed on your feet." Boss slapped him on the back.

Nathanial smiled up at Boss, did a double take, and exclaimed, "Whoa, you're blue!" And it was true. Every inch of Boss was blue. His skin was on the lighter side of the color, but his thick head of hair was such a deep blue it seemed black. His eyes remained the same chlorine blue and they shined down in humor at Nathanial.

"Yeah, it's a curse. But don't fret, you'll find your own color soon."

"Really?" Nathanial crinkled his nose at the thought. He wasn't sure how he felt about being a color like blue. It was a little too X-Men for his taste.

"You can take those cuffs off now," Boss said flicking one of Nathanial's ears. "And how about you open this Niche?"

Nathanial quickly pulled off his ear cuffs and put them in the box he had in his pocket. Then he licked his lips, rubbed his hands together and put one hand on the inside of the Niche edge like he'd seen Bunny do.

"Nothing's happening," Nathanial said after a few seconds.

"It's your first time, it might take a minute."

A minute passed.

"Maybe you should do it," Nathanial said dropping his hand.

Boss put Nathanial's hand back on the Niche. "You don't feel that?"

"Feel what?"

"The vibration."

Nathanial concentrated and only then did he begin to feel it. "Yeah, yeah there is a vibration," he said.

"Just grab it," Boss said dropping his hand off Nathanial's. "As if it's a substantial thing."

Nathanial squeezed his hand. Although the wall of the Niche was made of concrete, it began to give around his hand like clay.

"Now, pull," Boss said.

Nathanial did so and the door cracked open. "That's awesome," he said.

Boss helped pull the Niche wide open and went into the bright light within.

"Hey!" Nathanial called after Boss. "Wait! I can't get my hand loose!"

Boss stopped, looked back, shook his head, and returned to assist. "Drop the connection," he said.

"What?" Nathanial said pulling away as the wall began tightening, solidifying back into concrete.

"The Niche is open, the vibration is weak, just let go of the connection."

Nathanial stopped struggling and felt for the vibration again. He couldn't feel it. All he felt was his hand melding into the concrete and becoming stiffly a part of the wall.

"Ahhh, it's not working," Nathanial said forcefully tugging at his wrist with his free hand. Little crystals of gray began to creep up the captured wrist.

Boss took hold of Nathanial's stuck arm and said, "Hold still."

Nathanial held his breath. The spreading concrete stopped, then it receded. The stiffness in his fingers loosened and his hand slipped clear of the wall. He shook out his arm with a shiver and blinked away the little sparking lights that flashed in the back of his vision. "That was freaky," he said as an understatement.

"That's because you lost control," Boss said seriously. "Let that be your first lesson. Everything is made from the same substance at its core. You, me, and this wall, we are all held together by vibrating spheres that can sense one another. The spheres will either want to repel or attract, to make solid, liquid, or even gas. The trick for us is to know how to control that vibration. To do that, you must stay calm. Don't let fear or doubt guide your senses, and always stay in control."

Nathanial nodded. *Always stay in control.* Did that mean inanimate objects could be in control or was it his own fear he had to keep in check? Either way, he didn't like the idea of getting his hand stuck in a wall forever. It was not the best start to his first day as a sprite. Boss told his mother this was a trial period before Nathanial decided what to do with the rest of his life. Maybe he could choose to be human again if this all became too much for him.

Boss waved for Nathanial to join him out on the busy sprite floor. "Welcome to the Johnsonberry Transportation Hub," he said.

There was a marvelous organized chaos in front of Nathanial. Most the sprites seemed to be in a hurry to get somewhere as they swished by with luggage made from mint boxes or ring boxes or just boxes with little wheels attached to them. So many colors made up their skin tones, he wondered if even the Crayola crayon company could name them all. Nathanial ducked as a family of winged sprites flew over his head!

"This hub is thanks to a human factory that is both a pilot and a farmer," Boss said as they walked through the crowds. "A perfect combination for a travel port. We are on one of the high beams of his greenhouse. It's always safer to build where the humans won't think to look, even if they couldn't see us standing on the tip of their nose. It keeps us out of accidental stomping range, to say the least."

"Johnsonberry," Nathanial thought out loud looking around. "Do you mean Jake Johnson the pilot?"

"Probably." Boss nodded.

"His son goes to my school. Why do you call him a factory?"

"He produces jobs for the sprites. We use his animals for travel and we hop on to him when he goes to work, if he's flying to a desirable location. We've even altered the course of his day if enough sprites request a specific destination. Most sprites do still prefer to Niche hop, but that can take time and lots of organization."

"Bunny said my Niche goes here now. What factory used to be by my room?"

Boss looked down at Nathanial with a lifted brow. "That's what I was telling you about earlier. *You* were the factory. All the Niches in your town lead to Thatcherville. It was nice while it lasted, but you can never expect a human-based settlement to be forever. That's why the bulk of headquarters stays airborne."

Nathanial pictured the deserted town he had walked through with Bunny. His actions had caused that place to shut down?

Reading Nathanial's troubled expression Boss said, "Don't feel bad about what happened there. You were being taken advantage of as a factory. It wasn't right."

A loud bark startled Nathanial's attention away from Boss and over to where he found a line of sprites going through a gate with a beagle waiting behind it. The sprites were boarding the dog in orderly leaps and bounds, jumping from their positions on the ground all the way up to the beagle's back, and filing themselves into rows amongst the dog's hair that had been shaped to form seats. It all mimicked very well what you'd find on a modern-day airline, including the baggage handlers who secured the luggage using a giant net on the back just before the dog's tail.

"Whoa," Nathanial gawked. "Can I jump like that?"

Boss smiled at the spectacle and said, "Yes. It takes practice to get the landing right. I don't recommend trying it until you have a large, soft, space to practice."

Nathanial let his eyes travel along the line of

boarding gates. All sorts of animals had been retrofitted for a large number of occupants to ride: ducks, chickens, rabbits, rats, a baby goat, and a piglet.

"Are we going to ride one of these? How did the animals get up here if we are on a high beam of a greenhouse? How are we going to get down?" The consecutive questions spewed accidentally out, one over the other, as Nathanial seemed to be transformed back into his four-year-old sponge-absorbing-knowledge self. They stopped at a ticket booth and Nathanial waited expectantly for any answers that might come.

Boss's impatience reflected momentarily in his tense shoulders, but, to his credit, he took a breath and answered anyway. "These are all local rides. We're going too far for any animal to accommodate. As for how they got up here, if you are impressed with herding animals up ramps, then your mind's sure to be blown by what we're about to do. There's only one timely way to get where we are going and it's not by animal, factory, or Niche."

The sprite in front of them stepped aside and Boss leaned an elbow over the counter to address the ticket-sales sprite. She had porcelain skin, a white-and-blue striped mini-dress uniform, and a triangular white hat atop streaked purple hair.

"How are the West Winds looking today, love?" he asked her with a dashing smile.

The sprite, whose nametag read *Ivory*, smiled back and swiped her tablet. "Looks good for an afternoon glide. Are you interested?"

"Oh, yes, very interested… Oh, you mean in the flight! Well, yes we are." Boss chuckled as the girl giggled and her cheeks turned rosy.

Nathanial was surprised at the flirtatious banter. Boss nodded at him with assurance.

"Good news," Ivory said, her white teeth shining between dark purple lips, "I was able to shift some seats around to get you cushioned gliders at first gust, no extra charge."

"Wonderful," Boss said slapping a hand down on the counter. "I knew you'd be my lucky girl."

Ivory happily printed out the tickets. Boss took them with the exchange of gold and silver coins. "You have a beautiful day, sweetheart."

Nathanial stared up at Boss. Using flattery like it had an on/off switch was something he'd never seen before. One moment Boss showed visible frustration toward Nathanial and the next he was as cool as the breeze toward a stranger. It seemed a dishonest sort of personality quirk that only confirmed the mistrust Nathanial seemed to hold for the sprite.

"Another good lesson," Boss said glancing at Nathanial's expression. "Flattery is a wonderful tool to get what you want."

"I don't think that's a lesson specific to sprites," Nathanial murmured. He felt a deep aversion to all forms of deception. If he had to endure lessons about the finer points of manipulation, on top of his sprite training, he would be looking for a way out of this lifestyle quick.

WELCOME TO HYPERION

*T*he West Winds' cushioned gliders ended up being little more than leaves souped-up with thin moss liners. Nathanial was instructed to lay down in one. The attendant pointed a gun labeled *Web-o-matic* at him and shot a sticky white substance over his torso, attaching him and his backpack, that he had been instructed to put below his feet, to the leaf. A line of similar leaves adorned a conveyor belt, and Nathanial watched as Boss settled into the one in front of him.

"Good afternoon, everyone, and thank you for choosing West Winds Air, your only choice for a direct flight to Hyperion. Our gliders will be swooshing you from coast to coast today in just five hours," said a cheery male voice over an intercom. "We invite you to lay back and relax as we get ready for takeoff."

At that, the conveyor belt jolted into motion and the leaves began to move forward toward an incline.

"If you haven't flown with us before, there is no

need to panic," the cheery voice continued. "Your glider is aerodynamically designed to support the lightweight body of the hollow-boned sprite and travels smoothly along the west-bound airstream."

Nathanial narrowed his eyes. Was he fully a sprite yet? Did he have hollow bones? His leaf tilted as he began to rise up the incline of the conveyor belt.

"As you approach the air-shoot that will take your glider up to the 30,000-foot airstream, please refrain from moving until you've reached the cruising altitude."

The leaf glider just three places up from Nathanial leveled out onto a platform and suddenly shot up into the air. Nathanial's heart plunged into his stomach with anticipation.

"If you pass out during the flight, then a congratulations will be in order." The intercom voice chuckled. "Your flight may have just gone from five hours to five seconds."

Boss was at the platform and then he was in the air. Nathanial couldn't control his breathing. He was sure he was hyperventilating—he had read about it in a book about phobias. He pictured his frenetic body movement teetering the glider out of control upon its launch and smashing into the glass ceiling. The disturbing image escalated his breathing.

Nathanial's leaf leveled out and he stared momentarily into the blue sky above. He couldn't tell if there was an opening in the greenhouse roof or not. He swallowed with a dry sticky tongue in his mouth, and he heard the intercom say, "We hope you have a nice flight and we'll see you on the other side."

The pressure was insane. He wanted to scream, but he couldn't. He was up, up, up and out of the greenhouse before he could even compute if he'd passed the point where he'd feared an impact. The leaf edges around him bent downward with the roaring pressure. Nathanial could just see clouds racing toward him from behind stinging, squinting eyelids. He passed through the foggy cold and felt a sudden impact as if a train had hit him.

The glider curled up around Nathanial with the forward thrust and finally allowed him protection. With a commanding breath, Nathanial gulped down a gigantic swig of air. He felt a flood of chilled air fill his lungs and a buzz of lightness in his head. The green leaf in his vision faded from crisp and cool to deep and dark until his eyelids gave way to an uncontrollable weight that pulled them solidly shut.

Next thing he knew there were West Winds

flight attendants around him cheering. They cut the spiderweb-like restraints off his body and helped him to his feet.

"First-time flyer, eh?" one asked.

"Haven't had a black out in years," another said.

"Welcome to Hyperion," said a third.

Boss came up and put his arm around Nathanial, "Lucky dog," he said. "I wish I could still black out. What a boring flight."

Nathanial felt nauseous. He sat down on the nearest bench and Boss brought him a water from a nearby concession stand that was set up out of a walnut. He drank thankfully while observing the new surroundings.

This transport station was much smaller than the one at Johnsonberry and was more like what Nathanial had expected to see when he went through that first Niche with Bunny. It seemed they were inside a tree, since the floor had age rings like you'd find in a cut down tree trunk— and the smell was unmistakably woody. He saw squirrels and chipmunks around for the local rides. They darted in and out of burrowed holes that were scattered throughout the redwood walls, picking up a couple of passengers at a time.

"So what's the deal with this place?" Nathanial finally asked when he felt sure the queasiness had subsided. "Who's the factory here?"

"Hyperion," Boss said. "One of the few reliable factories in existence. It's where you'll take your courses. It acts as a school, hospital, housing, and marketplace, as well as this transport hub."

"It?" Nathanial repeated.

"You ready to walk?" Boss asked.

Nathanial got to his feet.

"Then allow me to show you." Boss held out his arm in a guiding fashion and they walked out through an open archway.

From the bent branch where they now stood, Nathanial put his hands on a woven vine railing and peered out in awe as Boss said, "Meet Hyperion."

Nathanial felt a sensation in his eyes that could only be described as joy, for allowing them to soak in such beauty. They scanned the natural bridges, like the one Nathanial stood upon, which crisscrossed and connected down the limbs of the tree. It was like standing atop the highest skyscraper in the world. The entire forest was of giant trees like this one, but none quite as high as where he now stood. Many hundreds of feet below was a blanket of green ferns that seemed impossible to ever reach.

"This is one of the tallest trees on the planet," Boss said. "It's a California coastal redwood that stands about three hundred and seventy feet tall and is more than eight hundred years old. It's the best kind of factory, in my opinion. One that we can rely on and we aren't hurting anyone by using."

"It's incredible," Nathanial said.

"Come on," Boss said with a pat on Nathanial's back. "You have school tomorrow and we still have to get your supplies."

"Tomorrow!" Nathanial exclaimed as they crossed the bridge toward a lower branch.

"Yeah, this semester has already been on a week. You'll be behind as it is."

"No kidding, I'll be behind. I don't know the first thing about being a sprite. I thought you were going to mentor me!"

"I will," Boss said calmingly, "but after your classes. And don't think of them as learning how to be a sprite. That's not what the classes are about. Everyone here was born a sprite, so that's not the focus. The classes are geared toward teaching what is inside each of us without care of blood abilities. This is a special school, even for sprites."

"Blood abilities?"

"Abilities passed down through sprite bloodlines. It's had a natural way of dividing sprites into different classes. Most sprites would rather stay within the confines of the class they were born into. For instance, a fire sprite will most likely grow up to mess with love lives and start forest fires, and generally enjoys causing havoc."

"That sounds about right," Nathanial said recalling something of the like.

"*Here* a fire sprite can take a course on how to harness those gifts for other uses or even shed them all together and pick up a new trade."

"That's cool," Nathanial nodded.

"It is," Boss said, shifting his head from side to side, "except a lot of sprites don't think so. There's always been some controversy around this school. It feels at times that the majority of sprites favor staying true to their heritage and think that to tamper with what is natural is shameful. It's a lack of initiative, if you ask me. It's people like Bunny who are the real heroes and deserve admiration, not recoil. When her blood trait kept her from accomplishing her goals, she decided to take action. Her plan to become a dust sprite revolved around a vision to use the dust in promoting sprite/human relations. She had this grand idea to start a tourism company and send sprites on human destination vacations, thinking it could open up their eyes by seeing how alike they and the humans were, but every loan officer she applied to for start-up funds denied her. She's still saving up for it, even if the only job she can get is in trash management. She'll keep selling her dust on the side until she accomplishes her dream. She used to be your wish sprite. Did you know?"

"Really?" Nathanial said uncertain as to what the implication of that was.

Boss nodded. "She tried to grant you several shooting-star wishes—and every eyelash you wished upon—but she was always denied her claim at the review process. It just pushed her to the point where she felt like she needed to make a change if she wanted to make a difference. She asked her sister to take over your case, feeling you would continue wishing your same wish until it became a ten-year wish. That would make it strong enough to be granted."

Boss smirked in remembrance and continued. "It was kind of sneaky of her, really. She kept all this information from me until after your hearing. She never even let on that she knew you. I came to her by your Niche for a little dust every so often through the years. She must have known I'd become pretty jaded working as your factory manager and didn't want to tip me off that she was going to help you if she could. She's a clever one, that Bunny, and she still keeps an eye on you to this day. You're lucky to have her."

This bothered Nathanial because he couldn't remember having any interactions with Bunny before yesterday. She sounded like someone he'd really like to know. What was it going to take to get his memories back?

They came to a stop at a set of clover-shaped doors. One had a picture of stairs, the other of a spiral.

"Want to take the stairs or the spiral?" Boss asked Nathanial.

"Er," Nathanial contemplated, "the spiral?"

Boss opened the door with the spiral, sat down just inside, and then he was gone. Nathanial peered into the dark. "Boss?" He mimicked Boss's movements and sat down. He realized he was on a slide and pushed off.

Nathanial spiraled down the smooth surface, only able to see his path occasionally as he slid past a window that was perhaps little more than a crack in the bark. At the end of eight rotations, he stood up dizzily and found Boss waiting.

"Haha." Nathanial chuckled. "That was fun. I've never seen a slide anywhere but on playgrounds. Makes it seem silly to use in a practical way."

"You're going to be saying that a lot around here," Boss said and led him on.

They entered a marketplace carved deep into the side of the tree. Large arched openings with the occasional twisted pillar opened the marketplace up to the treetop air. Colorful tented merchant stands lined the open archways while more permanent shops tucked themselves in hollows down the line of the tree. This allowed a curving walkway to form naturally through the center where many multicolored consumers happily meandered.

It wasn't long before Nathanial's curiosity pulled him toward a tent that twinkled with silver trinkets. He picked up a rather mystical looking magnifying glass. Its shiny handle had silver vines twisting up and around it.

Boss came up behind Nathanial and said, "Feel free to look around. I'm going in this shop here to purchase your supplies." He pointed just across from them.

"Cool," Nathanial nodded.

Boss took a step then hesitated. "Don't go too far."

"Sure thing," Nathanial said while examining his large fingerprints through the magnifying glass.

He wondered if the swirls of skin had changed at all lately. Did sprites even have fingerprints?

Boss went through the door marked *Scribble the Dribble,* and the merchant in the tent approached Nathanial. He wore a red-and-gold wrap around his dark head and neck, and his colorful silver-speckled clothes hung loosely off his body.

"Do you like the glass, my boy?" the merchant asked motioning to the magnifier.

"Yeah, it's neat," Nathanial shrugged, "I've never seen one so big."

"Ah, but you have never seen likes of this at all!" the merchant said.

"I've seen a magnifying glass before," Nathanial scoffed.

"This is no ordinary magnifying glass, my boy," the merchant said, putting a finger to the air. "Here, let me show you." He pulled out a green leaf the size of a notebook and laid it down in front of Nathanial. "Take a look at it through that special lens you hold."

Nathanial was skeptical, but he moved the glass over the leaf. Within the veins of the leaf, he could see thin green glowing movement. Occasionally there were tiny electric sparks that would jump from one vein to the next.

"Whoa," Nathanial said, bringing his head down closer. "That's wild."

"Do you know what it is you see?" The merchant smiled.

"Looks like circuits in a computer chip."

The merchant furrowed his brows, "That's human tech nonsense. This is real, boy."

"What do you mean?"

"What you can see there is what we all feel and control in our everyday lives." The merchant said bending toward Nathanial. "Those are the vibrations within all."

Understanding dawned on Nathanial. The merchant was talking about what he felt in the Niche; the spheres that made up all things. If he was to be a successful sprite, he needed to learn how to control these tiny elements without them getting control over him.

"With that glass you can seek out where the vibrations are strongest." The merchant said with enjoyment at Nathanial's obvious interest. "No more feeling around in the dark to grasp what you desire. You will be able to see it, and take control for yourself. Only three gold pieces, and it is yours."

Nathanial's expression dropped. "I don't have any money."

The merchants' expression mimicked Nathanial's disappointment. "Where are you from?" he asked curiously.

"Why, did I say something wrong?" Nathanial asked and put the magnifying glass down.

"You speak of circuit boards and money, not vibrations and coin. If I didn't know any better I'd say you were raised by humans." The merchant laughed uncomfortably loud.

"I will put the coin down for the boy," said a deep gruff voice beside Nathanial. "But not a ducat over two silver."

The laugh desisted immediately and the merchant said, "I said three gold to the boy and you offer two silver? That is an outra—"

"It is a traveled sprite you bargain with now, merchant," the growl interrupted, "not an Entry Schooling. I'd take the two silver before the boy discovers how your glass is merely a dolled up soda bottle bottom with a simple tap into that leaf of yours."

"Well, I...two silver, but...well, that barely covers the price of the handle!"

"Then wait for another Entry to come along," the man said, pulling Nathanial away. "Maybe the next one will be from a century family with the funds you desire."

Nathanial let himself be led away by the man, a little confused about what had just happened. He examined the heavy leather black boots beside him, up to a black-and-silver belt that seemed to be holding a concealed weapon—maybe a sword—beneath a thick long cloak. The hand upon his shoulder was gloved in black, but strangely had a silver ring on the middle finger with a coat of arms bearing crossed keys atop a sword that seemed to sparkle with diamonds. Nathanial finally had the courage to glance up to the man's face. His skin was deep green with black eyes and was shadowed by the hood of his cloak.

Nathanial stopped. He didn't trust this man and he felt fearful. Something from his lost memories screamed at him to run. He was afraid to speak as the black eyes turned upon him.

"Thank you," Nathanial managed to conceal his instinctive fear, "for standing up for me back there."

The man nodded and watched Nathanial glance back to *Scribble the Dribble* a few shops back. "I want to show you something," the man said and put his hand back on Nathanial's shoulder, pushing him on.

Nathanial's heart was pounding through his chest. He was almost out of eyesight from where Boss went for supplies. He stopped again. "I can't," Nathanial blurted out. "My mentor told me to stay close to the shop he went in back there."

The man forced a smile through his sneer. "It's just over here," he said handling Nathanial more forcefully.

Nathanial looked to the shoppers and merchants around him. They were taking no notice of them. He thought to cry out, but he wasn't sure if this man meant to harm him. Maybe he really did just want to show him something, but it just didn't feel right. They were coming to the end of the shops and Nathanial saw a hovering vehicle, like a silver convertible without wheels, at the path's edge in front of them.

Boss came out of *Scribble the Dribble* with a bag. He looked in both directions but couldn't see Nathanial.

"Where is the boy I left here?" Boss asked the silver trinket merchant.

The merchant scoffed. "Some Swartza came and pulled him away. Probably recruiting again."

"A Swartza?" Boss exclaimed. "Which way?"

Nathanial knew the man was taking him to the

vehicle now, and it was time to get serious about saying no. He pulled himself strongly away and said, "I'm not going anywhere with you."

"Afraid you don't have a choice," the man said. He grabbed Nathanial with amazing speed, and tossed him over his shoulder causing Nathanial's backpack to fly off and over the tree's edge. The man jumped into the open vehicle and threw Nathanial into the back.

Boss came around the marketplace's end just in time to see the vehicle take off. He dropped the shopping bag and dove out of an archway. What had appeared to be Boss's tailcoats a moment before, spread open into a pair of wings that carried him out into a grasshopper style of flight.

Nathanial was holding on for dear life in the backseat as the vehicle plummeted down the tree and swerved around its branches. He managed to look up for a moment and was relieved to see Boss on their tail. Boss's lips were calling something out to him but he couldn't hear over the roaring wind and the vehicles rumbling engine. Nathanial shook his head and pointed to his ears. Boss tucked in his arms and wings, speeding his dive through the fork of a branch. Nathanial covered his eyes, thinking Boss had hit the branch, but with his successful reappearance, Nathanial could finally hear something.

"Jump!" Boss was calling. "Nathanial, jump!"

Nathanial's gaping mouth expressed his distraught understanding. He looked to the front seat where his mad driver continued to swerve around and around the tree, getting ever closer to the ground. Nathanial swallowed his panic and jumped.

He was airborne, his stomach in his throat, and even with all the books he'd read on skydiving his mind was blanking out on him. His uncontrolled spin was about to get the upper hand on Nathanial's attempt to remain calm when Boss knocked the breath out of him with his catch. That was ok, though. Better to be caught by a winged man and lose his breath than continue falling alone with too much of it.

The vehicle took quick notice of its lost passenger and U-turned toward the pair of freefallers.

"When you hit the branch, ROLL!" Boss yelled at Nathanial and stiffened his wings outward to slow their fall.

Nathanial had no time to process. The vehicle was upon them. Boss pushed Nathanial away, allowing the vehicle through the open space between them. Nathanial hit a branch rolling. Dazed, he looked up and saw Boss a few yards down the branch, getting to his feet and looking for the vehicle. Instead, he found a door behind him and called to Nathanial, "Get inside!"

Nathanial wasn't sure if he could move after that fall, but his adrenaline told him to shut up and get up. He made a mad dash for the door. The vehicle came from below and positioned itself directly behind Nathanial.

"Get down!" Boss screamed.

Nathanial dove and the vehicle flew over him. Boss jumped onto its hood, over its windshield, and then he punched the driver. The vehicle rolled off the side of the branch.

Nathanial ran to the place it had disappeared and looked over. It was nowhere in sight.

"Boss!" Nathanial cried out.

Another minute passed with Nathanial pacing from one side of the branch to the other. Where could they have gone? Did they crash? Shouldn't there be smoke?

Boss landed behind Nathanial from somewhere above.

"Jeez," Nathanial cried. "Give me a heart attack."

"I thought I told you to get inside," Boss said

walking toward the door.

Nathanial followed asking, "What happened? Did you kill that guy?"

"No," Boss said, glancing at Nathanial and letting him go through the door ahead of him. "He got away."

"He got away? Who was he? What did he want? Why did he try to kidnap me?"

Boss looked seriously toward him, licked his lips, and took a breath. Nathanial anticipated great answers but instead he heard, "Let's get something to eat."

Chapter Four

A BUGGY NAME

*N*athanial sat at a wooden corner table in the dim light of a small restaurant drinking fruit juice and picking at his remaining fried potatoes. He glanced up at Boss who was at the bar having his tankard refilled. Nathanial quickly looked back down as Boss returned to the table.

"All right," Boss said after a large swig. He splashed the tankard down in front of him.

Nathanial was ready to hear some answers. Boss held his gaze and said, "That was the sprite you can thank for your lost memories."

Nathanial was dumbfounded. Boss pushed his hair back and continued. "I've been fighting the company he works for in legal battles all year. His employers insist on you being returned to your factory state. They are the reason none of us could contact you until you started showing signs of change. If you had gone another week without showing any sprite abilities, then they would have won the right to revert you."

Boss drank deeply in a moment of silence.

The words sunk in for Nathanial and he imagined how crushed his spirit would have been if he had been forced to return to his sterile confinement after having the taste of freedom. He was, for the first time, thankful for his pointy ears.

"So, if he lost the right to revert me back into a factory, then why is he after me now?" Nathanial asked perplexed.

"Word is he's gone rogue and has taken up a personal vendetta against you for escaping his grasp last year, but I don't know. He could still be working for headquarters and they just put that word out to cover their butts. Not every sprite is so hateful of humans that they'd be okay with kidnapping, and it's better PR for headquarters to wash their hands of this mess. Then again, maybe it's true he's no longer with headquarters and he *has* joined the Swartza. They've never been shy to flaunt their disgust of humans."

"Swartza?" Nathanial lifted a brow.

"An elitist group that puts sprites above all other living creatures," Boss explained. "The merchant who saw him seemed to think he was one. But anyway, we just need to keep you inside. I've let the local authorities and school staff know what's happened and told them to keep a lookout. I don't think he'll be trying to get you here again. He won't have the element of surprise anymore."

"Sorry, but I still don't think I understand," Nathanial said slowly. "If *by law* I can no longer be reverted back into a factory, then what exactly does he hope to accomplish by taking me?"

Boss took another drink and nodded his head saying, "I don't know."

Nathanial groaned.

"I'm going to find out though," Boss pointed a determined finger.

Nathanial considered again the question of why he had ever wished to be a sprite. Maybe this was a terrible mistake. "You told my mom that after this term we would decide what's best for my future. Was that code for deciding if I was going to keep up with this sprite thing or go back to being human? And if I could go back to being a human, does that mean I'd have to be a factory again? Would I lose my health?"

Boss rubbed his eyes and pondered a moment before answering. "Yes, you will have a choice at the end of the semester, but the changes you are seeing now," he pointed to Nathanial's ears, "and the changes that are yet to come—there is no stopping that. If you choose to go back to your mother, if you choose to live as a human, you'd still have to hide this new part of yourself. It's a hard decision either way. You are stuck between the two worlds, not being fully sprite and not being fully human. Both civilizations have a hard time being easy on those who are different, but I don't think it's something we need to be considering until after you've given Hyperion a chance. This place caters to those who are looking for an alternative to the norm." His gaze fixed on Nathanial before slowly turning introspective.

Boss slapped the table in front of them, guzzled down the remainder of his mead, and then barked, "but until then, we'll just stay focused on the task at hand. You have to be on your guard. Don't let anyone know you were ever human. Your true story must remain a secret. Make the kids think you belong. Yes, this is an open-minded school, but even the most open-minded person is a little prejudiced."

Nathanial furrowed his brows. He didn't like where Boss's third drink of the night was taking him and he didn't like the idea of having to lie.

"And you never know whose kid you might be talking to. Work hard, don't call any attention to yourself, don't run your mouth—and maybe we'll get through this," Boss said, wiped his mouth, then rose to his feet.

"Ok." Nathanial rolled his eyes. "Thanks for the vote of confidence there, chief."

"You're welcome." Boss patted Nathanial on the back. "Bedtime."

Boss led Nathanial into what he called an air-shoot. It was little more than a sprite-sized scoop in the bark that, when entered, felt like an entirely too-fast elevator shooting him skyward by means of wind propulsion. There were moments of dark and light exposing different floors. Though there was never a danger of falling out onto these floors, as the tube Nathanial traveled in only opened a crack to these sites, it still gave him a woozy lightheadedness. Finally, one after the other, they popped out into a hall full of dorms, and Boss guided him past several doors before stopping at room number 23. He reached into his pocket and pulled out a plastic baggie.

"Ok." Boss burped a little. "You're going to put your hand on this film when I open it for you." He pulled transparent plastic off a clear circular gel that was indented with the number 23. "Go ahead."

Nathanial stuck his hand over the gooey substance. "Ew," he moaned. "What is this?"

"It's your key," Boss said, pulling the remaining plastic off the gel. "Only you can open this door…

and any teacher...and me."

Nathanial looked at his sticky hand and watched as the goo melted into his palm and disappeared.

"Go ahead and open it like you would a Niche," Boss said gesturing toward the door.

Nathanial put his hand on the knob-less door and felt for the vibrations. His hand tingled and he pushed the door open. He had no problem releasing the vibration this time, which surprised him because he'd almost let the memory of becoming one with a concrete wall float to the foreground of his thoughts, but as the door opened so easily the fear had no time to manifest. He smiled triumphantly as he pulled his hand clear.

"Good," Boss said. "I've arranged for a student in your class to come get you in the morning. Get some sleep."

Boss started down the hall. "Wait!" Nathanial called after him, "where are you going to be?"

"I don't like sleeping this high," Boss said without bothering to turn back. "You can feel the wind rock the tree when you stop moving. I'm in the apartments at the base of the tree. See you tomorrow after school."

Nathanial went into the dark room and the

door closed behind him. He breathed in the smell of a forest drying after a day of rain. The ceiling slowly grew brighter in warm light as if it sensed his entry. The bed on his right was scooped out of a tree knot with thick quilts and colorful fluffy pillows piled inside it. A tilted desk with a stool sat against a circular window at the far end of the room. To his left was a wardrobe and dresser that reminded Nathanial of the wooden puzzle box his mom once gave him for Christmas. Not a single drawer or door was the same shape.

This was to be his room for the semester, at a sprite school that stood high within a giant tree in a distant land far away from the only home he'd ever known. A flush of nerves and excitement skittered within Nathanial. He hurried over to the window and flung it open. The fresh cool breeze filled his lungs and he counted to ten. Before his twelfth birthday he would have been having a coughing fit by now. In moments of stress, this was the kind of action he now took to calm himself down. It was true that his lack of recollection was irritating, but if he had wished for this sprite life, and if it was what granted his health, then he was thankful for that much at least.

Noticing a bag and a note on the dresser's top,

Nathanial went over to read it:

Heard what happened. I took the liberty of getting the rest of what you need. Had to guess on your clothes size. All you need to take to class is what Boss got you in the bag.

See you tomorrow,

Mr. P

Nathanial wondered who this mysterious Mr. P was, then curiously opened the cloth bag that was embroidered with *Scribble the Dribble*. He pulled out a pocket-sized notebook. On the bark-like cover, in gold stitching, were the words, *All I need to know is within*. He opened the book to the blank speckled pages and he sniggered, guessing he didn't need to know very much then. A white-tipped glass pen was stuck in the spine and there were occasional pocket pages that notes could be slipped into.

He set the notebook down and began opening drawers. There were underwear, socks, pajamas, towels, and nicely folded T-shirts—all of which were the same color, gray. He opened the wardrobe and found five matching pairs of dress pants, five white-collared shirts, and three blazers, each with a tree-shaped patch knitted on the chest that said *Hyperion*. On the floor was a pair of black rubbery shoes.

"Great…" Nathanial groaned. "Uniforms." He picked up the shoes and flexed them. Their soles had more wavy traction grips than he'd ever seen on a shoe.

Nathanial changed into a pair of the cotton pajamas and climbed into his pool of covers. His clothes were snug and he had to twist to loosen them up as he lifted his arms over his head. He stared at the warmly glowing ceiling for a moment then sniffed his underarm.

"Whoa, I *have* to find a shower in the morning," he said, putting his arms back down.

He watched as the ceiling began to fade and his eyelids became heavy. He was asleep before he could remember to worry that he was about to start a whole new school in the morning.

There was knocking on the door. Nathanial opened his eyes, freaked out, and fell out of bed. He popped back up quickly and looked around in the morning's light. He had no idea where he was. He'd just been dreaming about being stuck in the middle of the ocean in a small dinghy and was afraid he'd just fallen overboard.

Nathanial noticed an oval mirror by the door and pulled at his pointy ears. "Oh, right," he said, remembering his just as unusual real circumstances and pushed his unkempt hair down over the points.

The persistent knocking climbed up Nathanial's last nerve. He grumpily went over and flung open the door.

A small, wide-eyed, white-haired sprite boy in the school uniform stood there looking up at Nathanial. He seemed quite bothered and said in almost a whisper, "You're not dressed. We'll be late!"

Nathanial groaned. "Where are the showers?"

"You can't take a shower!" the boy squeaked. "We'll be late!"

"I don't care if I'm late, I can't start a new school smelling like rotten eggs," Nathanial said as he went to find a towel in the dresser drawer.

The boy rushed in past him, searched the dresser, found a spray can in the bottom drawer, and circled Nathanial with the cloudy contents.

"Hey, hey, hey," said Nathanial wafting the smell of pine away and pleading with the frantic little sprite. "Calm down!" He coughed from the overwhelming aroma.

"Get dressed, I'm supposed to show you to class. My name's Spassel. You're Nathanial, but the other boys won't call you that. They'll find a nickname for you. I could never give out a nickname. I'm not that creative." Nathanial got dressed as the boy continued to ramble. "But that's not to say I'm not clever. Being creative uses a different part of the brain than being clever. I'm youngest in the school. I had to pass a test to get accepted. That has to say something for my intelligence. Did you take a test? You're a late entry, so you must have. They don't usually let anyone in after a term has begun."

"Ok," Nathanial said, sliding on the flexible shoes and feeling just ready enough to get on with it. "Show me the way."

Nathanial snatched up the little notebook off the dresser, slid it into his pants pocket as they exited his room, and then tucked in the white-collared shirt as they walked down the empty hall. Looking down at his pant legs scuffing at his ankles, Nathanial horridly realized all his clothes were as ill-fitting as the pajamas.

"Most of the boys are already getting to class by now," Spassel said to the emptiness. "You should really set your alarm to be early, not on time." They went down a set of stairs at the end of the dorm. "Early is on time. On time is late."

They walked through an archway at the end of the stairs and the new sight pulled Nathanial's attention upward. He tripped, distracted by his awe.

It was like he had walked into a massive wooden pagoda. He had never been inside one in real life, but had researched them when he dreamed of one day traveling to Asia. Two separate stairways spiraled up the circular tower in opposite directions around one another in beautiful symmetry for several stories.

"Oh, man," Nathanial said looking to the overwhelming heights. "Tell me our class isn't at the top of that."

Spassel looked up. "No, not the first class, but there are shoots that go to the top if we needed it. There are shoots to all the levels. It takes some time to learn the best routes to classes. You'll get the hang of it."

Just then, a girl came through the large entryway to Nathanial's right. She looked pretty normal in her gray knee-length skort and three-button blazer until her wings sprouted from their perfect concealment and she flew up the center of the tower.

Nathanial jumped back from her sudden flight

and said, "I guess we could just sprout wings and fly up!"

Spassel shrugged and said, "I don't envy flyers. Too much maintenance required. Come on." He turned left up the nearest set of stairs.

They made another left at the apex of the twelve steps and walked down a hall full of opened doors. Beyond each were students settling into the classrooms. It was then that Nathanial noticed most of the kids didn't have crazy colors like the adults he'd seen at the transport stations. In fact, he would consider himself tan against this lot. Their skin was so pale it was almost translucent.

Spassel reached the end of the hall and entered the last classroom. Nathanial took a deep breath, brushed his long bangs back to one side, tugged his inch-too-short blazer sleeves pointlessly toward his wrists, and entered the room.

Everyone who had been chatting, settling in, and pulling out tablets stopped to stare at the new kid in town. Nathanial gulped.

Spassel took a seat in the first row and waved Nathanial over to join him at the empty desk behind him. Nathanial tried to act cool and unbothered by the twenty or so pairs of eyes on him and made his way to the desk. The chatter slowly started up again and Nathanial glanced around at what the students were putting on their desks as he sat down at his own. He noticed his wooden desk was attached to the floor and looked as though it had grown there with root-like feet and twisted branch legs.

Spassel turned around and whispered, "Do you have your tablet?"

"Uh," Nathanial raised his brows and almost asked, *like an iPad,* but went with the safer option of: "No."

"It's ok. You can access the portal through the desk flap," Spassel said as he swiped the top of Nathanial's desk to reveal a matte screen that glowed with the symbol of a redwood tree expanding out of a kite-shaped shield and the words *Hyperion Student Portal* swirling over it. "There's an access point in your room's desk, too, but you should really get a tablet so you don't have to rely on the portal for doing your schoolwork. They're all hard-tapped, but they'll give you a key if you want to set up your own tablet so you can be portable."

"Cool," Nathanial said, surprised. "You guys are pretty high-tech!"

"What?" Spassel asked with a crinkled nose.

Nathanial remembered the market man saying tech talk sounded human and tried to cover. "I mean, I just didn't realize I should have brought my tablet." And for the first time in his life he was experiencing what it was like to fear prejudice and have to lie to protect himself.

"Really? I don't know anyone who doesn't take theirs everywhere with them."

Nathanial looked around and caught a couple of eyes still looking at him. He was surprised to see the school uniforms surrounding him weren't so *uniform* after all. Many of the kids had different shaded blazers, some were even short-sleeved or more like vests. Not all the girls wore skorts either; many had pants similar to his own or even shorts. One kid had twigs poking through about every inch of his clothing and hair.

Nathanial swallowed hard as he felt his scrutiny reflected and turned back to Spassel. In a whisper, he said, "Look, I really don't like sitting in the front of a classroom."

Spassel slumped with disappointment and said, "Well, all the century kids sit in back. I guess you could sit over by Mila if you want."

Nathanial followed Spassel's eyeline to an empty desk a couple of rows back, next to a girl described, from Nathanial's limited experience, in two words as punk rock. He was a little shocked by her look, having never seen such a thing in person and forgot to blink as he accidentally checked her out.

Mila had lots of necklaces bunched up between the two top unbuttoned shredded collars of her shirt and blazer. It seemed like every piece of her uniform had met a similar fate from scissors, only to be pinned back together with assortments of crab pincers, twisted metal, or colorful string. The black leggings under her gray skirt met with high boots, and the rings on almost every finger passed silkily through long black razor-cut hair. Her eyelids and irises were purple and there was a shade of maroon within her lips. There were deep purples in her skin tone around her hairline and fingernails.

Nathanial knew he had been staring too long when Mila's sharp eyes looked into his. He quickly turned back to Spassel and said, "I'm ok here, thanks."

"Alright, alright, alright!" said the enthused voice of a teacher as he entered the room, closed the door and threw down a big bulky bag on the front desk. "Who's ready for week two of General Sprite Knowledge?"

The class only vaguely showed attention, but this did not discourage the orange-tinted professor. He smiled happily, tugging at his corduroy suit while his wispy straw-colored hair trailed after his every swift movement. He swiped the wooden wall in front of them. It lit up with the reoccurring tree in a shield symbol and the words *Hyperion Student Portal* blazed into life.

"A small recap on last week's topics," the professor said as the wall changed in unison with the images on Nathanial's desk. "I introduced you to your new home, Hyperion, and a brief history of settlement. Why we chose it as the place to have such a unique educational experience, away from the normal influences of development. The possibility for each of you to discard your birth-given abilities and shed your logical societal placements, and setting the goals of tapping your personal preference vibrations rather than falling into the line with your blood traits."

The professor continued his lecture with unwavering enthusiasm, and with each topic there were pictures flying past the screen with descriptions and diagrams around drawings of the sprite anatomy. Nathanial was sick with the feeling he had already missed way too much.

"I'm sure all of you have noticed by now we have a new student," the professor said out of nowhere about thirty minutes in and he turned his attention to Nathanial. "My name is Professor Thicket. Please come up to the front of the class and introduce yourself."

Nathanial remembered how this went from the year before. On that occasion, he was finally joining public school after enduring years of boring, lonesome online courses. When he stood in front of that class, he had been thrilled to tell them all about how he'd been stuck sick in his room his whole life and was totally excited to be joining a normal group of people for a change. Now he was walking up in front of a group that was anything but normal and he wasn't supposed to say a thing about his true self. He cleared his throat and smirked as he reached the teacher's desk.

"My name's Nathanial. You can call me Nate or Nathan," he said nodding and throwing his head back to clear his bangs.

"Nathanial?" said a big, slate-colored, kid in the back. "That's no name for a Hyperion." The guys around him smirked and nodded in agreement. "Neither is Nate or Nathan. Sounds hoaxy to me." He looked at his fellow classmates with sly concentration. "But we can play on the name. You're Nat from now on. What'd you make of that, Nat?"

Nathanial glanced around to the students who jittered with anticipation for his reaction. He thought it sounded a little buggy, but he nodded and said, "Yeah, that's fine."

The kid grinned wider and sat back down saying, "Yeah, that's fine."

"What's your name?" Nathanial asked with a strong tone that surprised the group and threw the attention excitedly back to the kid in back.

"Bron," he said, and looked hopeful for a comment on it.

Nathanial nodded and said, "Yeah, that's fine, too."

The class laughed, Bron quite louder than the rest.

"Alright, alright!" the professor said, slapping Nathanial on the back. "Thanks *Nat*, welcome to Hyperion!"

Nathanial sat back down. He figured Bron was much like the Brad of his last class: a rich kid with nothing better to do than stir up drama. He knew how to handle him, thanks to the rough friendships with Brad and Jason, but he hoped he wouldn't have to. He'd already spent too much time picking his battles with bullies, and knew how to gain their respect, but he wanted things to go differently this time. This was a new school with new chances for friendship.

The rest of the class went on without any more

intermingling. Nathanial was racking his brain over the professor's discussion on how to discipline and clear the mind of all thoughts in order to hear the calling within. The idea was to listen for one's own inner passions rather than keep to the beat society had drummed out for them, but it all sounded a little kooky to him. Clearing his mind didn't seem possible. Every time he thought he was getting close, he'd get excited and think about how well he was doing. That in itself was a thought, and it would string into another thought about what exactly would happen once he did clear his thoughts.

The professor demonstrated the process after watching the class meditate for fifteen minutes. Nathanial noticed a slight pigment change in the professor's cheeks. He worried that the professor may be holding his breath for too long. But then the room darkened and the professor began to hum and glow.

The oohs and ahhs of the class gave Nathanial the impression he should be impressed. Having read about bioluminescence in creatures such as lightning bugs or jellyfish, he wouldn't have thought the sight so unusual that it called for such admiration, but it told him that it must be a rare sight to see in sprites.

A bell gonged from somewhere in the distance and the room's light was restored. Everyone applauded the professor who returned to normal.

"'Til next time," Professor Thicket said with a bow.

Everyone rose to file out of the room. Nathanial could tell by the clustering that cliques had already begun to form. Girls gravitated to girls, and boys elbowed or pushed each other in jest. Nathanial was the last one out of the room and he was thoroughly surprised as a giant arm wrapped around his head and pulled him suddenly into a walk down the hall.

"Hey, Nat!" said Bron, pulling Nathanial amidst a group of three other grinning guys. "You know, I got a feeling about you, Nat; a feeling you will be one of the few at this guppy school that can go the mile, you know what I'm saying."

Nathanial noticed Spassel was keeping an eye on him, but also keeping a distance. Bron saw Nathanial's glance and called over, "Hey, Spaz. You can buzz off. I got this one." And Spassel hurried off beyond the crowd ahead.

"So, what d'you say, Nat? Want to be one of the big boys?" Bron said tightening his arm around Nathanial's neck.

Nathanial really couldn't care less about being

a part of the *big boys,* but he really didn't want his head separated from his body just then either. "Sure," he groaned out from beneath the huge armpit.

"See, I knew you'd be tap," Bron said letting Nathanial out of the hold. "This is Sil, Kale, and Jax." He pointed to the three tall sprites from left to right who dominated the hall beside them. Sil had ruffled red hair, Kale's was black with flakes of white, and Jax had shockingly blue spikes atop his chiseled brow. All their other jock-like features were fraternally similar.

They acknowledged Nathanial with nods and he reciprocated the gesture. They entered the pagoda-like tower and moved up another flight of stairs.

"So, you have wings spit?" Bron asked examining the back of Nathanial's blazer.

"No," Nathanial said apprehensively, watching the approaching ledge that jutted out beyond the stairs railing.

"Aw," Jax said, spreading his wings. "You sure about this one Bron? I don't think he can keep up," and he rose up the tower.

The other two scoffed and followed suit.

Bron turned to Nathanial pointedly saying, "First vibration you tap will be to sprout a pair, got it? Until then, take the shoot behind the waterfall before the next flight of stairs, make a left on exiting, and run down the hall until you come to a gargoyle. There you make a right where you can take a spiral down. The classroom will be on your immediate left at the bottom. If Jax makes it there before you, this won't be an easy semester for you. Got me?"

Ok, so this guy was a little more intense than Brad. In fact, Brad was really just a teddy bear wasn't he? Bron's pupils had just engulfed his entire eye sockets before shooting back into place. Nathanial nodded his understanding with fear that he hadn't truly understood those directions at all and received a farewell push in the direction of the next set of stairs.

Mr. P

*T*he waterfall was more like a trickle down the bark of the tree, and the gargoyle looked more like a dog with rabies, but it didn't take Nathanial long to find himself at the bottom of the spiral slide and jumping into the classroom like he'd just been running from a monster. Bron's threat was monster-ish, after all.

With Brad and Jason, the bully game was always more of a mind game. They tried to embarrass kids publicly, and if you couldn't stand up to the rhetoric, the verbal abuse would only worsen. Nathanial had become pretty good at standing up for himself against this type of attack. Pretending the words didn't hurt, as well as throwing a good insult or two back, could take away some of their power. Physical abuse, on the other hand, that was something he had no experience with, and now he wondered if it came to it with Bron, would pretending there was no fear still be enough of a deterrent?

Spassel came into the room behind Nathanial

and did a double take.

"How'd you get here so fast?" Spassel asked, astonished.

Nathanial tried to catch his breath and said, "Bron told me a shortcut."

Spassel's face fell and he said, "Oh," before sulking over to a seat at the front of the room.

Nathanial instinctively went over and sat behind Spassel, which obviously surprised the kid.

"Aren't you going to sit with Bron?" he asked, a little hopeful that he wasn't.

"Um," Nathanial said as he watched who was entering the class. "You said the back was for century kids."

The same students from the class before were taking their seats in very much the same order they had earlier. The room was laid out similarly, but where the other room didn't have windows, this one had a curvy crack opposite the entrance wall that allowed some natural light to assist with the illumination already glowing from the ceiling.

Then Jax walked into the room. He made eye contact with Nathanial and broke into a laugh. He strode over amusedly.

"How in fire sprites blazes did you get here before me?" He asked.

Nathanial shrugged and said, "Guess I don't

need wings to keep up."

Jax nodded. "Well, get your speedy butt back here with us before Bron sees you up here with the smoochers again."

Uck, was this really happening? Did he *have* to go sit with the bullies? Nathanial looked over to Spassel who had turned back around and was acting very interested in his tablet. It was hard to believe he was thinking of refusing Jax to stay close to a chatty A.D.D kid, but he did want it to be a choice and it just didn't feel like one. What would Boss say? Hadn't he said, *stick to yourself*? He really shouldn't be choosing anyone to sit with. Sadly, this was not at all about his choice, but about what he needed to avoid, and a confrontation was not an option. Nathanial slowly rose and followed Jax to the back of the room.

Bron came in with the rest of his pack and looked pleased with himself when he saw Nathanial sitting by Jax.

Everyone was settling in when the teacher entered the room. Nathanial wouldn't have pegged this guy for a teacher. He had a yellowish-green tint to him, slicked-back green hair, and jagged pointed ears. He wore black jeans with suspenders that came up over his red button-up shirt.

It wasn't until the teacher said, "Mornin',

everyone," with a Brooklyn accent that something clicked in Nathanial. He knew this sprite. This was the *Grit the Gook* sprite! Not everything was clear about him, but he remembered seeing this sprite putting phlegm into a vial and hanging it on his jumpsuit. In fact, he was pretty sure the teacher's name *was* Phlegm. Nathanial wasn't sure if he liked this teacher and his tightening fists seemed to agree.

"I was going to give a quiz on last week's material, but you can thank the new kid for its postponement," the teacher said, nodding to Nathanial in the back. "You can call me Mr. P, by the way."

The century kids around Nathanial sniggered. He thought he heard one of them whisper, "Mr. P-thetic.". It was obvious they had no respect for Mr. P, and with his own uncertain feelings about the teacher, he felt uncomfortable with his possible agreement with the cruel kids.

"I'm your vibrations teacher," Mr. P continued to Nathanial. "We went over the basics last week, so you need to stay after class for me to run you through it."

"Aw, Nat, that dregs," Jax whispered in an unsympathetic voice beside him.

Nathanial nodded his acknowledgment toward

Mr. P who turned and launched the screen behind him.

"Now, as I was saying at the end of last week—about letting the vibrations get hold of you, it's rare that the circumstance is ever too much for a stronger sprite not to pull you out of." He turned away from the picture of a sprite caught in a wall and looked toward the class reminiscing, "I knew this one kid who got stuck so deep in a factory mucus cavity that it took me twenty minutes to dislodge him." He laughed as the class reacted in disgust. "A week later, he was findin' gook in places he didn't even know he had creases!"

"Unnecessary." Bron groaned.

"Anyway," Mr. P said wiping a laughter tear from his eye, "this week we are concentrating on the vibrations in beasts of burden, and I always say the best way to learn is to do! Well, I think that's the first time I've said that, but anyway, it's true." Mr. P swiped the screen back to its bark form. "Everyone can go to lunch early." The class murmured in excitement. "I've arranged to use the P.E. court an hour before your lesson there, so, off with you until then, except for you." He pointed at Nathanial.

Everyone got quickly to their feet and began filing out the door with smiles. Bron gave Nathanial a slap that took his breath away. "Blows for you," he said before exiting. Once Nathanial was the only student left in the room, Mr. P went over and shut the door.

Nathanial didn't know what to expect. He wasn't sure if he was anxious or angry as he watched Mr. P approach him.

There was a moment where they just looked at each other. Nathanial got the feeling Mr. P was annoyed with him, too.

Nathanial finally blurted, "What?"

Mr. P looked like he was ready to give Nathanial a practiced rant. "What?" he mocked. "What, you ask me. Look at me. I'm a teacher at freagin' Hyperion and you ask me 'what'?"

"Yeah, what?" Nathanial shrugged, his hostility bubbling up through his cracked memories. "You act like that's my fault."

"It *is* your fault!" Mr. P shouted. "You were my factory and you had to go and make a selfish wish that changed the lives of everyone who operated around you."

"Selfish?" Nathanial shouted, too. "Who's the selfish one here? If it weren't for you, I could have had a normal life from the start. Maybe I was born with a weak immune system, but if it hadn't been for you, I would have grown stronger a long time ago!"

Nathanial didn't know where that knowledge came from, but he knew it was true. He blamed Mr. P for the situation he was in just as much as Mr. P blamed him for his.

"I told you I don't make the decisions on where I work or for how long. I can't help that you made such a good factory! But out of all the wishes you could've made on your exchange day, you chose to be a sprite! What were you thinkin'?"

Nathanial opened his mouth to retort, but then didn't. Why had he wished to be a sprite? He felt there had to be a very good reason, but there was still a horrible blur in his brain and he hated it.

"I...I don't know," Nathanial finally said with his anger melting into sorrow.

This seemed to cool Mr. P's anger as well. His converging brows relaxed and he dropped his cold stare. "Well," he said softly, "guess it doesn't matter why now. It just ain't an easy situation we have here. If word gets out that you are the factory that turned sprite, it won't matter how many friends Boss has here."

"What are you saying?" Nathanial asked, becoming fearful.

"It'd cause an uproar. Factories becoming sprites ain't an easy thing for folks to swallow.

Already those involved are gettin' their turn on the chopping block. After the abduction of the sprite who allowed your exchange, the courts erased the names of everyone else involved from the record, but all that does is keep new haters from knowin' us."

"They kidnapped Gem?" Nathanial said as a flash of her sweet timid face appeared in his mind's eye. He knew she had helped him and was partially responsible for granting him his health. "But why? I don't understand what the big deal is. So what if a human becomes a sprite?"

Mr. P sighed. "I'd like to say it's just headquarters trying to cover up their embarrassment of losing such a profitable factory but…" He looked unsure about getting into the subject. "I think Boss's fears that the Swartza are involved is more than likely."

"He was saying they're an elitist group. So, what?"

"I'd say elitist verging on a cult. When people believe as strongly as they do, there's no reasonin' with 'em. Their belief in sprites' superiority over humans is a matter of fact. Sprites capacity to wrangle the vibrations is the only proof they need on that. Humans are no better than any other factory, meaning you are as important to them as this tree or a dog or a flea on that dog."

"And so the fact that I've become a sprite is, what, offensive?" Nathanial guessed.

"More than that," Mr. P said. "If you do well, it could be the crash of their entire system. It would mean that factories are just as capable of great things as sprites; that the vibrations in all things are as important as their own. It would make it immoral to use humanity without consideration. It might even give strength back to the rebellion against the Crossing Treaty."

"Crossing Treaty?" Nathanial repeated.

"Yeah, it was a compromise signed way back to end a sprite war. It's what stopped humans from seein' us and also stopped us from havin' to negotiate with them, and, like with any compromise, that meant neither side really got what it wanted from the deal, but it had to be done to stop the sprites killin' each other. It's been up for repeal many times. Not all sprites like using humans the way humans use cattle, but everyone is too afraid to touch it, 'case it starts another war." Phlegm said waving his hands off the subject. "But to the point of what I'm gettin' at, stay away from those century kids."

"Ugh." Nathanial threw his hair back out of his face. "I don't need you to tell me that. They're obviously a bunch of creep-a-zoids."

"And their families are most likely to be Swartza."

"Oh, great," Nathanial groaned. "Why's that?"

"It's in their name. They were born to uppity ruling-class families that've been in power for centuries and still occupy half the seats in government, but they are kept in check by the elected half. These kids probably think you're somethin' special comin' to Hyperion a week late. They're going to ask you a lot of questions if you stick around 'em."

"Well," Nathanial thought about the precious goal of keeping his head upon his shoulders, "what if I can't avoid them? What should I say?"

Mr. P licked the front of his teeth while in thought. "Tell them a recruiter found you in Fayetteville. You stunned a bunch of kids with a forget-trick when Bunny picked you up right?"

Nathanial recalled that strange moment with a twist in his gut and could see the frozen faces of his schoolmates. Nathanial nodded.

"Then that'll work. Your people are Fay, if they ask. Fayetteville is a little sprite town notorious for their forget-tricks. It's always easiest to keep a lie that's close to the truth."

"Okaaay," Nathanial said, lifting a brow.

"Now, let's get you to the cafeteria. The century

kids always grab their lunch to go, so you should be in the clear for now, and I'll tell your other teachers to keep them away from you as much as possible."

"You can try," Nathanial shrugged, "but I'm sure I'll have to deal with them myself, in one way or another."

Chapter Six

FLYING SQUIRRELS ARE NUTS

*T*he cafeteria had a pretty cool feel to it. Even though it was an interior space, there were thick branches twisting up the center of the circular hollow, and wavy seating alcoves tucked into the cozy rim. Most of the branches had stairs spiraling up around them to reach other sitting areas, but Nathanial could see some of the flyers eating their lunch even further up, amongst bare limbs that weren't outfitted with tables or chairs. There was plenty of light streaming in through dozens of misshapen windows and best of all, plenty of food choices at stations scattered against the far wall.

Nathanial walked between two long knotted tables with stump benches until he could get a good angle on all the food station titles. There was Middle Mutton, Mex Mix, China Chow, Southern Style, Sea Faring, Dough Bowls, Sandwich Stop, Soup and Salad, Gruel and Mash, Fire Forte, Hyperion Specials, and Delectable Desserts.

Nathanial's nerves had been rattled all day, so he

thought he'd be safe in the Soup and Salad section. He went over to the station and groaned. There was no chicken soup, potato soup, or even tomato soup. Instead, there was lizard soup, nutmash, and pinecone porridge. He moved on to the salads. No Caesar salad, no iceberg lettuce, and no Cobb salad. Just clover greens with little yellow flowers, petal picks, and pistil mix.

Nathanial moved on to Dough Bowls, intuitively thinking of bread bowls, but found instead bowl-sized olives that were stuffed with cheeses, meats, and he presumed the white bobbles mixed in were the dough. At the Mex Mix station, there were corn kernels stuffed with chopped rice and spicy sauce. He didn't feel much like spicy. He was hopeful at the Southern Style station, but then he couldn't be sure it was fried chicken that fell to pieces with the tongs' pinch. He decided to just grab whatever the Hyperion Special was and take his chances. Besides, he could always stock up on desserts if he didn't like it.

Yellow honeysuckles taller than him dripped clear juices into a glass container at the drink station before him. Nathanial took a peach pit cup and filled it from this fountain that was labeled *Honey Water*. He placed it onto the tray with the colorful variety of foods that came together as the special. He was only looking around for a place to sit for a second when he saw a hand fly up in the air and wave to him. It was Spassel. Nathanial went over to join him at a small table in the center of the room.

"Hey, Spassel," Nathanial said, taking a seat.

"Hey!" Spassel said, munching away with a smile. "Did Mr. P tell you all about vibration catching? That's all he spoke about last week. Everyone found it kind of boring, though, because everyone knows how to catch a vibration. How would you open a Niche otherwise? I did find it kind of interesting about how *vibration* is a dated word. Did he tell you about that? How we used to not be able to use the tap to see them, so we only felt them. I guess it was a pretty big deal when we first were able to *see* the vibrations. I don't know why we didn't rename them. But what would we call them, you know? It's still something I think nobody can really understand even if they say they do. *A mysterious force that moves through and connects everything.* What do you think?"

Spassel had spoken so quickly, Nathanial had to stare intently at him in order to process the information in real time. "Midichlorians," he said quickly, as if answering a movie trivia question.

Spassel laughed and said, "That's funny. Where

did you come up with that?"

Explaining George Lucas and the *Star Wars* universe didn't seem like a good idea so he shrugged and said, "I don't know," then looked down to his adventurous food.

Nathanial took a two-pronged fork from the utensil cup in the center of the table and skewered a purple square off his plate. Nibbling the edge of it, he was pleasantly surprised at its amount of flavor. It was a little nutty, but somehow as savory as a steak.

"Mmm, this is good," he said and then put the entire thing in his mouth.

"Yeah, the special usually is," Spassel said, finishing the last bite of his own. "It's all fresh from the Hyperion gardens. Not sure how they pack so much punch into vegetable-based meals, but somehow they can make a squash taste like chicken! So what do you think beast vibrations is going to be all about? We're too young to drive, don't you think? I mean, I know this is supposed to be an advanced school, but surely they wouldn't bring in an animal this early in our education! We had a Chihuahua at home for a little bit, but the thing was always yelping and chasing its own tail. We could never get it to go straight. I fell off it once and it almost licked me to death! Dad drove it down to Beverly Hills after that and I never saw it again."

Nathanial snorted into his honey water.

"We thought about getting another animal for a while, but we couldn't decide which type would be best. Dogs have a good sense of smell and usually don't get lost, but we'd already tried that. We thought maybe a pig would be good, seeing as they always find food and you won't go hungry on a road trip. Then we considered a raven, since they have amazing camouflage abilities that could come in handy when we need to hide from the relatives after a family gathering, but, I don't know, they have a bad rap. We just Niche hop for now... anyway," Spassel continued with hardly a beat between thoughts. "If you like the lunch special, you should come early for breakfast. They always have a tasty Hyperion breakfast and that *is* the most important meal of the day. It would also help you get to class on time."

"There's breakfast?" Nathanial said suddenly interested. He had been wondering about that.

"And dinner!" Spassel nodded as if obviously so. "The cafeteria is open from dawn 'til dusk. Classes start and end at different times throughout the day, so it's never too crowded in here. Our lunchtime is usually set with all the other newbies, but since we are a little early today you can see some of the older students here."

Nathanial looked around and noticed some budding colors around him. No one was a full-blown color yet, but there were some pinks and sky-blue teens hanging around each other.

Nathanial tried to smoothly phrase a question about this observation without sounding like he didn't know *anything* about it.

"What color do you think you'll be?" Nathanial asked confidently, in hopes it sounded like a normal question.

Spassel looked a little surprised and uncomfortable but softly said, "I'll probably be yellow, like my parents." He waited to be judged, but when he didn't see any such response from Nathanial, he asked, "What about you?"

Nathanial shrugged. "I don't know."

"So you're hoping to change your blood then?" Spassel's eyebrows shot up and he leaned in.

"I guess."

"That *is* why most sprites come here from all over the world, even if they don't say it out loud for fear of judgment," he said looking around. "Funny how a school so open and encouraging about blood change still has students so afraid to talk about it. Maybe I'll change my blood, too!" he finished in an excited whisper.

"Anyway…" Nathanial cleared his throat. He barely understood the subject of blood change, only having heard briefly about it. He could tell it was normally taboo from Spassel's whispered tones and from the story Boss had told him about how Bunny could only get a job in trash management after having done it. For this reason, he sought to change the subject. "Where is our next class?"

"In the arena! Are you ready?"

Nathanial finished his last bite of food and said, "Yeah, let me grab a cake to go and we can head out."

Spassel led Nathanial up higher in Hyperion than either of the previous classes. They went outside to enter an air-shoot that exposed Nathanial to the frightening sight of a long possible fall through the gap in the shoot. He kept both arms firmly to his sides and averted his eyes from the nauseating height.

Once they reached their destination branch, the only thing left above them was the transport station and the blue sky. Below, he could see many of the bridges that connected branches toward the marketplace.

"So, where's this arena?" Nathanial said not believing they could possibly go any farther.

"We're here," Spassel said as they took a corner around a truck-sized tree knot.

Nathanial marveled at the grand scale of what was carved down into the branch before him. It was a stadium-seating field with moss covering its oval center floor and obstacle courses spread throughout. They jogged down what had to be more than a hundred stairs to get to the bottom and Nathanial hoped there was an air-shoot back to the top. A few of Nathanial's classmates had already gathered near a jungle gym–like structure and Spassel was heading toward the punk rock girl, Mila.

Nathanial stopped as soon as he noticed the intimidating girl, but when Spassel turned toward him with expectation, he went and joined them.

"Nat, this is Mila," Spassel said introducing them. "She's my rec partner. Most groups have four, but we were the last two. Maybe coach will put you with us!"

Nathanial couldn't help but notice Mila's lack of enthusiasm.

From above, Nathanial heard the familiar laugh of Bron. He looked up and saw him and his posse coming down for a landing. They stopped on different posts of the obstacle.

"Hey, Nat, how'd your private lesson with Mr. P-thetic go?" Bron said jumping the rest of the way to the ground in front of him.

"Oh, you know…" Nathanial shrugged. "As well as you'd expect."

"I'd expect pretty dreg," Jax said, making the jump next.

Kale laughed and said, "Oh, scat, here he comes now," and swung down off his post, followed quickly by Sil.

Nathanial looked around Bron's broad shoulders and saw Mr. P walking toward the group.

"Looks like we're all here," Mr. P said after counting the clustered sprites before him. "Just need one more," and he whistled loudly by sticking two fingers in the corners of his mouth and blowing.

A flying squirrel the size of a school bus glided down from the tree branch above and landed in front of the group. Just about everyone did a duck-and-scream maneuver as it rushed toward them. Mr. P stuck his hand up in the air and let the squirrel sniff it. He closed his eyes and the squirrel blinked. It then lowered its head so Mr. P's hand was between its eyes and let its own lids fall shut.

"Now I've made the connection," Mr. P said

opening his eyes and looking to the group. "It's all about feeling for the vibrations, just like opening a Niche, but we aren't controlling the animal so much as communicating with it. Who wants to try?"

Nobody looked particularly anxious to do so and all seemed to be in disbelief that they were even asked the question.

"Just kiddin'," Mr. P snorted. "Everyone, get on aboard."

The class felt this was a much more reasonable request. They began springing like fleas from the moss floor and up to the squirrel's back. Nathanial's anxiety grew as he saw he was about to become the last one left on the ground. He knew Boss had said to wait for a soft place to practice this jumping technique, and sure the moss beneath him was as cushy as any gym mat, but he didn't want his first go to be in front of a class of experts. He looked to Mr. P for some kind of guidance, but instead got a head gesture that could only be interpreted as, *Well, go on!*

Nathanial gawked up to the dauntingly high destination, bent his legs, held his breath and pushed off with all his might. It was not a graceful sight. Hands and feet were flailing in the air as he turned upside down before crashing into the group of students amidst the squirrel fur. The kids he clobbered were grunting and pushing him while the surrounding ones were laughing hysterically. Bron grabbed Nathanial by the shirt collar and yanked him up.

"You're a funny guy aren't you?" Bron said, clearly thinking Nathanial was making a joke, and set him down beside Jax.

"Yeah." Nathanial gulped and gave a crooked smile. "Totally on purpose."

Mr. P landed at the front of the group. "K, now, everybody get a good hold. We're about to set off."

Nathanial watched everyone sitting cross-legged and wrapping strings of fur around various limbs. Some kids seemed more safety conscious than others, as they'd have fur tied around both legs and both wrists. Then there were a couple like Bron who just wrapped one arm up into the fur. Nathanial watched Mr. P turn to face forward on the squirrel's head. Nathanial knew they were about to take off. He quickly wrapped both arms in as much fur as he could muster.

The squirrel jumped up into the air and was off. It was not a pleasant sensation for Nathanial. It knocked the air out of him several times. He couldn't tell much of what was going on as the squirrel ran along branches and jumped from place to place. Occasionally there was a sickening feeling of being airborne as they glided down toward adjacent trees. It was all very bumpy and rough. There were sudden stops and sudden starts. Nathanial began to feel motion sickness.

What is it? his voice rang in a sudden memory.

It's ginger root, answered a girl's accented voice. *The sailors use it before they get their sea legs. I think I'm getting mine now, so you can have this bit I was using.*

"Aliya," Nathanial whispered to himself. He was just barely able to picture her: her dark kind eyes, scattered freckles, and curly brown hair. Mostly he wanted to remember her smile, but he couldn't picture it.

The squirrel came to a stop. Nathanial was thrown back into his current situation; everyone was untangling themselves from the fur. They were back in the arena.

"I'm sure some of you are wonderin' why we just went for a joyride," Mr. P said, standing and turning toward the group. "Not every sprite has a beast at home. I wanted everyone to know what it feels like. Did any of you pick up on the vibrations?"

A few of the kids nodded; most didn't respond.

"Usually a passenger won't bother catching the vibrations, but, everyone, wrap your wrists in the fur again," Mr. P said, showing them by example.

Everyone in the class bent down and grasped the fur beneath their feet. Nathanial did so as well, even though he was anxious to get Mr. P alone to ask what he knew about Aliya. He was excited to start remembering her. She felt important to him, and he knew Mr. P should know what happened to her. That idea worried him as well. Boss also knew Aliya, but he hadn't mentioned her. He definitely felt she was someone that should have been brought up to him by now.

"Can you feel it?" Mr. P searched the group for a response.

Nathanial didn't feel anything but an itchy arm from the scruffy fur and his heart racing from the memory flash. He pushed his arm deeper until his palm was on the skin of the squirrel. It was strange to feel the heat of a living thing under him. Then there was the breathing; how everything beneath him moved up and down. He heard his excited heartbeat growing louder in his ears and he realized it was way too fast. But then he noticed the quick thumping was more in his head than in his chest. He could see a sparking red heart melding with a flashing blue heart in the blurry dark of his unfocused eyes. Was this the rhythm of the squirrel's heart he felt next to his own?

"Nathanial," Mr. P said. "You feel it."

Nathanial snapped out of it. The entire class was looking at him.

"Oh, Mr. P," Bron spoke up. "This here's Nat," and he slapped Nathanial on the back.

Mr. P nodded. "Gotcha. So *Nat*, what were you just thinkin'? Your eyes were dilated. That's one indication of a sprite in tap," he explained to the class.

"I don't know," Nathanial said, shrugging. He ran his hand back through his windblown hair. "Guess I thought I heard its heartbeat."

"Good," Mr. P said, "that's a good piece of advice. An easy way to find a vibration in a beast is to try and find the heartbeat."

Just then a woman's voice called up from the mossy ground below. "Hey, Mr. P! Your time's up. These kids are mine!"

"Hold your rodents there, Coach Pectin, I'm wrappin' it up!" Mr. P said and turned back to the class. "Anyway, next time you go for a ride with your folks, I suggest you try catching a vibration or two. It will get you ready for drivin' yourselves one day. Nat's had a good start. Listen for the heart!"

The class started jumping down and Nathanial thought he'd catch Mr. P to ask about Aliya, but he sprung up to the next tree branch before Nathanial took a step.

Unable to chase after him, the only option left was to make the long jump down behind his classmates.

THE HYPERION GLIDER

Luckily, most of the class wasn't looking this time as Nathanial attempted another novice escapade. He had decided to slide down the side of the squirrel rather than jump like his former companions had. He lay down on his tummy and grasped onto the fur. The plan was to slowly let the fur slide through his hands until he softly reached the ground. The execution, however, had no regard for the plan. Nathanial slipped down the first half of the squirrel in quick jerky spurts, as the hair was never long enough to keep hold of for more than a second at a time. The second half of his descent didn't even have a chance for grace. The squirrel was no longer under anyone's influence and it decided to take off. Nathanial was forced to let go and he fell flat on his back.

Nathanial lay still for a moment, staring up at the squirrel as it skirted up the above branch, and he wondered again why he had ever decided to put himself through this. He turned his head and saw Mila giving him a quizzical look as the rest of the class gave its attention to the coach. He rolled over and pushed himself to his feet.

Coming up to the rear of the group, Nathanial forced his ears to tune in to the coach. "Enough of this vibrations mumbo-jumbo, let's talk about where the real strength of sprite comes from," she said with peacock pride. "It's right here in our bones!" She slapped her chest. "Everyone, change into your sweats, get in your groups, and meet me at the pinecone! New kid," the coach said pointing over to Nathanial, "you're with Spaz and Mila."

He heard Spassel's little voice say, "yessss," somewhere within the crowd as Bron laughed and shook his head.

Spassel appeared with a smile and said, "Knew it! You'd have to be with us. Come on. We'll get you some clothes and I'll show you where the pinecone is."

The group clustered around a pile of T-shirts, shorts, and strange rubber gloves. The gloves had the same wavy grips on their palms as on the soles of the shoes Nathanial wore. When he put them on, they molded perfectly to his hands.

It was a little weird the way everyone changed in front of each other. He guessed it didn't matter since the boys and girls all had gray undershirts and shorts on, but it still felt odd.

The pinecone they walked toward after dressing was three times Nathanial's height and would have been obvious enough to find without Spassel's gracious assistance. The coach reached it ahead of them, and skittered up its whole height in three monkey-arm swing moves.

From the top she shouted, "See that! Nothing but arm strength. You have to learn to use the lightness of your bodies and build up strength in your limbs. Caty, you try," she said as she pointed at a girl near the front with a white ponytail. "Your group will spot you."

Caty took her turn attempting to jump and pull herself up the pinecone brackets using only her arms. Nathanial saw Bron and his buddies getting bored and eyeing him. Bron jerked his head toward Nathanial in request that he join them.

Nathanial sighed and said to Spassel, "Be right back," and went to join Bron.

"Hey, man, sorry about your group," Bron said, with an insincere chuckle.

"Yeah, getting stuck with *the weakest length* and Mila the Skilla is a tough draw," Kale added holding his stare on Mila.

"I'm sure I'll make due," Nathanial responded. He felt uneasy with Kale's creepy eyeing of Mila. It looked both hungry and repulsed.

"I'm sure you will," Bron said, quickly brushing away the dull topic to get straight to his true agenda. "Look, me and a couple of the guys saw something on that pointless ride through the pines of Mr. P-thetic's. What room are you in?"

"What?" Nathanial asked, surprised by the question. What did something in the trees have to do with his room number?

"Your room number, spit."

"Ugh…" Nathanial had to think about it and was afraid he had forgotten. He looked at his hand and remembered the number twenty-three sinking into it the night before. "Twenty-three?"

"Perfect," Bron said, slapping him on the back. Then he walked forward for his turn to scale the pinecone.

Nathanial watched Bron make it to the top in two swings and wondered what he was getting pulled into with this guy.

Nathanial was last to attempt the pinecone. The gloves gripped great and kept him from slipping off, but it took him several swings to reach the top. The class moved on to other obstacles, and, as the lesson progressed, so did Nathanial. He wished he'd had it before he'd tried to jump on that squirrel. He caught on quick and started to stick his landings. He even made it to the top of a fallen branch in a single jump where it was taking others two. A couple of times he noticed Mila staring at his triumphant expressions like she was trying to figure him out. By the end of class, she still hadn't said a word to him.

Spassel, on the other hand, was very talkative and, unfortunately, very clumsy. He'd make a big speech about how to do the next obstacle and then overshoot it or trip on it.

When the coach called for everyone to stop and head for their dorms, Nathanial was actually disappointed. He liked getting the hang of something. He might not be able to clear his mind, but he could clear this obstacle course in no time.

Nathanial changed back into his school uniform, not bothering to button his uniform shirt, and headed toward the arena stairs at the tail of the group. He looked to Spassel who was limping beside him and asked, "So three classes a day then, huh?"

"Yeah," Spassel said cracking his neck, "but tomorrow is a different rotation. Today were all the required classes. Tomorrow we have the electives."

Nathanial nodded, wondering what he might expect from a new set of classes, but thought he might ask Boss rather than Spassel, and knew he was supposed to meet him after classes anyway.

"Do you know how to get to the bottom of the tree?" he asked, remembering Boss was staying in an apartment down there.

"Whoa," Spassel said wide eyed, "what do you want to go all the way down there for? Most sprites don't leave the canopy of Hyperion. There isn't anything below the marketplace until you reach the bottom and there's only private residence down there."

"I'm supposed to meet someone. Another teacher."

"You having private lessons?"

"Yeah."

"That's neat. Well, I guess the fastest way to the bottom is the glider."

Nathanial didn't like the sound of that. "The glider?"

"You can sign one out on the dorm level. Besides that, you know how you were asking for the showers this morning?"

Nathanial looked over at the nerve of Spassel's insinuation.

"Yeah," Spassel nodded to the knowing look, "you really need one now."

Nathanial swung by his room to grab a towel and a set of the casual clothes Mr. P had left him in his room, which consisted of a gray short-sleeved shirt marked with the Hyperion logo and a pair of loose brown pants. Spassel pointed him to the showers at the end of the hall and they went their separate ways.

The bathroom was the first place he'd encountered so far that didn't use the manipulation of wood to form its facilities. Slate rock had been inlayed along the walls and floor to divide the space into three showers and four toilet stalls. A row of water faucets jutted out from the rock wall to his left and seemed to drain along a gutter in the floor.

It took Nathanial a minute to figure out how to work the shower. He stood there in his private stall and stared up at a four-pronged root that protruded out from a small hole in the rock above his head. Just when he was thinking he'd hate to have to hunt down Spassel to ask him how to work the water, he finally spotted a hand-shaped hollow in the rock before him, revealing dark wet redwood within. When he put his hand into the strange hairy texture of the wood, he could feel the bark within it start to grasp around his palm. It became soaking wet and then water started to flow from the roots above him. He pulled his hand free, shook it out from the creepy feeling of momentary suction, and washed it off quickly before dousing and scrubbing the rest of himself with a handful of amber soap from the provided dispenser. Luckily, the water seemed to have an auto-shut-off after about ten minutes, because Nathanial was not going to put his hand back into the hole *after* a shower.

Spassel had told Nathanial the glider checkout room was just a couple of hallways down from the showers, and it was easy enough for him to find after throwing his dirty clothes back into his room. Mustering up the nerve to ride the thing wasn't as easy. Nathanial signed a disclaimer, and possibly his life away, to a rat-faced teen with an authority complex whose patronizing shirt badge said *Student Helper, Here to Assist,* while his smug face said the opposite.

"Okay, so this is wha-cher gonna do," the buck-toothed teen said. Nathanial's feet dangled off the ground while the teen buckled Nathanial into a contraption that hung from the ceiling. "You're gonna lean with the tree, see," and he pulled his arms into his chest and leaned. "Like this. The tree is circular so you're always pullin' right, see?" He kept his body leaned to the right and waited for Nathanial to acknowledge. Nathanial nodded and gulped. "You just keep your arms in, pull your legs up when you come to any overgrowth above the branches, and keep leanin'. Got it?"

Nathanial nodded, then shook his head and said, "You know what," he searched for the buckle to release himself, "I think I'll just take the stairs."

"Stairs!" The teen laughed so loud Nathanial winced. "Only if you want to be down by tomorrow afternoon!" And he pulled a lever that opened a hole in front of Nathanial.

The contraption—and so too Nathanial—began to move forward on its ceiling-strung wire system. Nathanial could see the glider wings just outside the hole he was about to exit.

"No really," Nathanial said insistently. "I don't need to go down. Maybe I'm not supposed to go down. Boss didn't tell me to go down. Maybe he's coming up! You know what, do you have a phone or something I could borrow."

But the teen was laughing too hard to answer and just waved Nathanial out of the hole.

Nathanial looked up and saw his harness click into the leaf-constructed glider. It swayed in place for long enough to allow Nathanial the horrible luxury of fully grasping what he was about to do.

The glider dangled by two opposing wheels pinching a vine-like cord. The cord was strung along a spiraling path of tree branches. Nathanial looked past his feet and to the ground hundreds of feet below. He wondered if he was about to pass out again.

There was a *click* noise and the glider began its natural relationship with gravity. It started down slow. Nathanial pulled his arms tight into his hyperventilating chest and lifted his legs over the first bushel of ferns and pine needles. But it wasn't long before gravity had the upper hand in the relationship. Nathanial had no illusions of control over his rapid descent. It didn't matter how much "leaning" he attempted to do, the glider would sway back and forth any time the cord's path straightened between the giant branches. He eventually gave up on leaning at all and could do nothing more than hold on for dear life—and scream.

Was this what it was like to ride a roller coaster? If so, he was seriously reconsidering next summer's amusement park trip he had planned with his mom. Last summer, they celebrated his new-found health by visiting grandparents that had only ever seen his face by computer chat, and that was glorious, but his mom wanted to increase the excitement scale for the next vacation. They had thought a fun park would do the trick. Unfortunately, Nathanial was discovering that the experience of things doesn't always play out the way that one imagines. He'd need to get his mom back to the drawing board on summer vacation ideas.

Nathanial couldn't decide if it was worse with his eyes opened or closed. When the glider finally started to slow, he opened them again. He was coming to the bottom of the tree. His hair was blown back and knotted, his face was red, his eyes were stinging, his ears were ringing, and he had little cuts on his upper arm from some pine needles he had failed to lean away from along the way.

Boss was waiting for Nathanial where the glider came to a stop. The amused look he wore was not helping, as another Hyperion student helper unbuckled Nathanial's harness. He took two wobbly steps toward Boss and hoped his hateful expression was sinking in, but Boss's smile did not waver.

"Nice ride down?" Boss asked coolly.

Nathanial continued his glare.

"I was pretty sure I told Spassel to send you down," Boss said repressing a laugh.

"You didn't," Nathanial said shortly.

"Oh, well. Glad you took the initiative."

Boss noticed the little specs of red blood on Nathanial's arm. His expression wavered and he walked over to the glider counter, opened a small bamboo box, and took something out. He pointed at a group of gray hoodies with Hyperion patches on them that hung just behind the counter and the student helper handed him one. He walked over to Nathanial.

Dabbing the small cuts dry with a ball of smashed-up leaves, Boss handed Nathanial the hoodie and said, "Put this on. It gets cold during the evening."

Nathanial took the clothing, not softening his expression toward Boss just yet. Boss was obviously a tricky sprite in need of a thorough analysis. He slipped the hoodie on, then noticed the zipper was missing, but as the green teeth of each side touched, they melded together to close the hoodie up.

"Whoa," Nathanial watched amazedly. "Is this hoodie magnetic?"

"Similar principle as magnetism," Boss nodded. "The opposing sides are built with vibration materials that want to naturally bond." Boss watched Nathanial open and close the zipper-like hoodie for several more seconds before saying, "Let's go," and he waved Nathanial away from the tree.

WHAT'S LOST IS FOUND

athanial followed Boss through a large thicket of towering ferns, under some decaying leaves, and out into an open patch of moss. Turning to Nathanial, Boss pulled a sheathed knife from his back pocket and held it out toward him.

Nathanial gazed untrusting at the offering and asked, "What's that?"

"Bunny's birthday gift to you last year."

"A knife?"

"It's called a battle blade."

"Why would I need a knife?"

Boss dropped his arm and looked to the sky as if to ask for patience. His request seemed to be granted. He looked back at Nathanial and said, "I believe this blade saved your life last year. Without it, you would have been lost, captured, and reverted back to factory status without a hearing."

Nathanial took in a breath, preparing to question, but Boss held up a hand and shook his head. "Just listen and maybe you won't have so many questions, okay?" He put the knife into Nathanial's hand. "It's not what it appears to be. Only three blades like it were ever made and they're more than six hundred years old. They were forged in a time when growing powers were spreading across the globe and the dynamic of the world was changing. The western Europeans and the Spanish humans were expanding into what they called the New World, and the sprite ruling class of the time, headed by a monarchy, influenced those humans to benefit our own migration. The battle blade was designed for a human to use through the will of a sprite. Whichever general was backed by the sprite authority would surely be victorious in battle with that blade. It was the means by which sprites controlled the fate of the world."

Nathanial looked down at the blade skeptically and examined the gold and silver carvings of a dozen armored men frozen in a spiral attack around the smooth hilt.

"However," Boss continued, "after years of bloodshed from war after war, the battle blades were eventually lost within the chaos. Soon after their disappearance, the Crossing Treaty was signed and sprites washed our hands of the affairs of men. A council was established in place of the monarchy and an agreement was made to use humans only as factories rather than as pawns to control the giant world around us." Boss rolled his eyes, "Or so the government tells the people, but you can trust that the day we use porky-pine quills in pillows."

Nathanial smiled a little at the unlikely analogy then asked, "So…what am I supposed to do with this again?"

Boss held Nathanial's amused look for a moment then allowed himself to smile, too. "Yeah," Boss said, "I don't think you'll be changing the world's fate any time soon either, but it's still a pretty cool thing to learn how to use if you're ever in a pinch, right?"

Nathanial shrugged, liking Boss's mellowing attitude and said, "If you say it kept me from getting lost last year, then I could definitely be open to learning more about it."

"Good, because honestly," Boss said seriously, "I think you're going to need it."

Boss proceeded to show Nathanial how the knife guided him the year before. Boss took Nathanial's hand, held it palm up, and, with the blade point facing down, he dropped the knife over Nathanial's hand. Nathanial screamed, closed his eyes, and without the strength to pull out of Boss's grasp, anticipated pain. However, none came. He peeked through squinting eyes at the knife hovering a millimeter away from stabbing his open palm. This sent another recollection of Aliya to the forefront of his mind. She had seen him do this and she was as amazed at it then as he was now.

Boss said, "Say 'Brujula'."

"Bru-chula?" Nathanial repeated and flinched as the knife twirled vertically then glided down like a feather to lay flat in his hand.

Boss smiled, pleased. "If you ever need directions, now you know what to do."

Nathanial bit his lip and blurted, "Who's Aliya?"

Boss's expression immediately fell. He obviously hadn't expected that and hurriedly faked a nonchalant answer. "Just a girl who went for a hearing the same time you did."

"I keep thinking about her. Do you know where she is? I'd like to talk to her."

"Mmm," Boss said through pursed lips. "She's pretty far away right now. I don't think there's a way to reach her. Anyway, you need to concentrate on yourself right now. Build up your sprite abilities. You've got a long way to go."

"I'm actually pretty good at obstacles," Nathanial said, defending himself, "and I felt a flying squirrel's heartbeat today."

He waited for Boss to acknowledge how good

that was for his first day of sprite school, but he didn't get what he was hoping for. Instead, Boss said, "Are you staying away from trouble?"

Nathanial curled in his eyebrows from the implication and said, "Yes."

Boss eyed him suspiciously.

Nathanial thought about confessing his fears of the century kids' persistent attempts to get to know him, but didn't want to hear the lecture that would surely follow it.

Boss took the knife from Nathanial's hand and began flipping it from palm to palm. He then threw the blade high into the air, shouted "Espada," and watched it grow gracefully into the length of a sword. Boss caught the handle and wielded the shining metal in several fighting style strokes before stopping to see Nathanial's reaction.

"Whoa, who are you again?" Nathanial said bursting out in astonished laughter.

Boss smiled and lowered the sword saying, "Your mentor, apparently."

"Well, teach me how to do that and all I'll need is a suit of armor to go with it."

"Believe it or not, lots of sprites still carry swords," Boss said while sheathing the blade. Astonishingly, it reduced back to knife size on entering the sheath. "One of the many dangers sprites face when out of the cities are big animals that want to eat them and a sword has a way of deterring hungry tongues."

Nathanial grimaced at the imagery and said, "Yeah, I guess it would," and he took back the knife that Boss held out. "So what else does a battle blade do besides act like a compass and grow into a sword?"

"Its complete abilities depend on the wielder, so I won't be able to tell you everything it's capable of. The answer to that is within you. *But,* I know it can be a shield," Boss pointed to the blade. "Hold it out in front of you, parallel to the ground."

Nathanial held the sheathed knife out in front of him.

"Like this," Boss said pulling Nathanial's arm straight and positioned the knife so he held it where the hilt met the sheathed blade. "Now say, or you know what," Boss backed up and looked at Nathanial hopefully, "just try thinking *shield.*"

Nathanial lifted an eyebrow, looked at his hand holding the battle blade, and thought *shield.* Nothing happened.

Boss nodded and said, "It was a long shot, but you should be able to control the battle blade with your thoughts eventually. It's still in Spanish mode right now but it'll get a feel for you after a while.

Maybe you should take it up with you for the night and talk to it."

"Talk to it?"

"Yeah," Boss answered seriously.

Nathanial sighed and followed as Boss led the way back toward Hyperion. He looked for a place to put the knife when he felt the mini notebook in his pocket. He pulled it out and put the battle blade in its place.

"So, Boss," Nathanial said opening up the empty notebook, "I'm assuming you got me this notebook to put school notes in, but you do know the school has, like, this computer network I can access with all the class notes already in there?"

"First of all," Boss said pointing a finger at Nathanial, "it's not a computer network and don't let anyone hear you talking like that. The portal is entirely organic. The information travels through nature's electrical currents—no wires involved. Secondly, do you have a tablet?"

"No..."

"No, you don't. So, if you need to remember something you heard once amongst the piles of information that's going to be dumped on you over the next few weeks, and you are not near the Hyperion Portal, what are you going to do?"

"Ok, ok, I got the point. You don't have to be

such a butt about it," Nathanial said grumpily and put the notebook in his free pocket.

"Speaking of the portal, you should use the one in your room to call your mom tomorrow. It's too late on the east coast to try tonight," Boss said looking at the dimming sky, "but it should be fine if you do it first thing after classes. It's easy enough to figure out. Just tap the *AV* symbol on the screen and think about your home phone number. It should connect."

"Really? And do you have a phone number in case I wanted to contact you?" Nathanial asked, thinking how nice it would have been to call Boss before he jumped on that glider.

"Sprites don't need phone numbers. You'd just think my name and my apartment tablet would vibe me, but I don't carry one around. Best way to reach me is through tap messaging, but we'll save that for another day."

They reached the base of Hyperion and Nathanial looked up its monstrous height.

"You can take the air-shoot back up," Boss said. "And when you come down the glider tomorrow," a smirk was forming and Nathanial narrowed his eyes, "you might want to think about using the brakes a little."

"What?" Nathanial's shoulders fell and Boss

laughed.

"I'm sure the glider kid knew you were an entry sprite and thought it would be funny *not* to show you the glider controls. Look for the two handles above you tomorrow. Pulling the one on the left leans the glider left, pull the one on the right to lean right, and pull them *both* to slow down."

"I'm going to kill that jerk!" Nathanial shouted.

"Well, don't be too rude or he'll give you the jinky glider."

"There's a jinky glider?" Nathanial gulped.

"Just watch your temper." Boss winked.

Nathanial was still fuming during his air ride back up to the dorm levels. All he was thinking about was how to tell off that rat-faced glider sprite without potentially fatal repercussions. He had made it all the way back to his room's hallway without once thinking about what was in his immediate potentially painful future until it was smack in his face.

"Nat, there you are! We thought you were flaking out on us, spit." It was Bron and his whole gang standing in front of room number 23.

Nathanial's heart stopped. He had completely forgotten Bron had asked for his room number earlier that day.

Bron walked toward Nathanial and put his arm around his neck. "Ready to go check something out?" Bron said with a rough shake.

"Sure," he croaked and went with him down the hall.

The group took a long air-shoot up the tree and stood out above the arena. Nathanial knew the sprites were looking for something they had spotted while riding the flying squirrel, but what it was or why they wanted it was information they enjoyed withholding from him.

"I think we started on that branch," Sil said, pointing to the right up above them.

Everyone, excluding Nathanial, spread their wings and flew up to the branch. Kale looked down at Nathanial and said, "Well, little spit, you gonna keep up this time or what?"

Nathanial looked around, saw a small knot between himself and the high branch, ran toward it, jumped, grabbed the knot and—with both hands—pulled himself on top of it so he could then jump again to the branch where the boys waited with gleeful anticipation. It was a little tricky climbing without the gloves he'd worn during P.E., but he managed it.

Bron applauded and shouted, "All right!"

Kale nodded, saying, "Not bad."

Jax turned away unimpressed, teased his spiky blue hair and said, "Yeah, we all know he can jump. Let's keep going. Sil, we flew over to that tree next, right?"

Sil confirmed and the group headed to the end of the branch. Again, Nathanial had to watch as the group glided to the adjacent tree. Nathanial thought he could jump this distance, too, but it would be a rough landing. It wasn't that the branch was so far, but it was high. It hung over the branch he currently stood on so missing it wouldn't be his death, but he wasn't sure for how long he could keep up with a group of flyers. Shaking his head and holding his breath, he took the jump. He rolled upon landing and managed to get to his feet quite quickly. No one was there to applaud him this time. The group was already making their way to the next branch.

Nathanial looked back behind him. He had just left Hyperion. He wondered if leaving school grounds was allowed and he considered turning back. If he did, what was the worst thing Bron could do to him? Tease him for sure, some scaredy-cat taunts maybe. If he didn't turn back, what would happen if he got caught? He could just explain he was new and didn't know the rules. Nathanial was very curious about what the bullies were so eager to find and he'd already gone this far. He decided to keep going.

It didn't take him long to catch up, but it was tricky enough that he wondered if it *was* possible for him to grow wings and if that was something he might want.

It had been another fifteen minutes or so of tree branch-hopping before Nathanial noticed it would soon be too dark to easily find his way back. He wasn't sure how much longer they would search before calling it quits and he was just about to speak up when he thought he saw a shadow pass behind them. Were they being followed?

"No guys, we've already looked over here," Jax complained.

"I know," Sil exclaimed, "that's because I am sure it's here. Somewhere around here, I know it!"

"You know," Kale cut in, "I do think it's on this level, but I'm pretty sure it was back on Hyperion. The squirrel turned here, crossed back over, and started up around this point. That's when we saw it."

Sil slapped a hand to his head and said, "You're totally right! Let's go back over."

Nathanial took this as happy news. They were headed back to Hyperion. Nathanial followed them to one of the lower branches of Hyperion, which was still an eye watering one hundred feet off the ground. Sil yelled, "There it is!" and Nathanial sighed a breath of relief at the prospect of his journey's end. But then he saw what Sil was flying toward. It was his backpack from home— the one he'd lost off the marketplace balcony when that sprite had tried to kidnap him!

Sil dug the backpack out from under the twigs and dirt it had been half-buried in. He flew with it back over to the group and handed it to Bron. "You were right, Bron," Sil said with a horrible smile. "It has to be a human's! Look at the material and the logos!"

Bron's smile was just as horrific as Sil's. He put his hand on the zipper and looked up to his admirers. "This could be the break we've been hoping for. This confirms a human has been brought to Hyperion and that the Swartza are right! The council disgraces our school by allowing in this factory trash. If the backpack tells us who the human is," he licked his lips with the thought, "can you imagine? The Swartza would be so pleased with us, they'd let us into Swartza High for sure!"

"I say we don't tell the Swartza when we find out who the human is. We should just catch the human and take it to her directly," Kale said menacingly.

"It will be the proof she needs to bring her doubters back to the cause. She'll probably anoint us on the spot!"

Sil and Jax cheered excitedly.

Nathanial gulped and started picturing what he had in his backpack. Was there anything in there that could give him away?

Bron started to pull open the zipper.

"Hold up a sec," Nathanial burst out and waltzed straight up to Bron. "Let me see that."

He took the backpack, opened it and searched as quickly as he could for anything that might have his name on it.

"What do you think you're doing?" Bron said snatching the backpack away again.

Nathanial knew playing the tough card wouldn't last long with a sprite a head taller than him, but it had been worth the risk. He didn't see anything that would give him away.

Then there was a scream from behind them. Everyone turned to see Mila running toward them, but it was her pursuer that commanded their attention. The first word to pop into Nathanial's head was: *dragon*!

Chapter Nine

AN ILLEGAL GIFT

*B*ron and his flying bunch of monkeys were up and onto the nearest dragon-free branch before Nathanial had even registered what he was really seeing. It wasn't a dragon, of course, it was a salamander, but from its size, it might as well have been a fire-breathing monster from the pages of lore. It was slimy and spotted and fast! It ran after Mila like an alligator going after its evening meal.

Her panicked expression was almost upon them and she screamed, "Don't just stand there, run!"

Nathanial didn't need to be told twice. He darted toward the trunk of Hyperion. He saw Mila jump to the adjacent branch and he did the same. The salamander reached the trunk, then skirted up and over to the branch he and Mila were on.

Nathanial feared that running would not do the trick, and he recalled what Boss had said about deterring hungry tongues. Nathanial reached into his pocket and pulled out the battle blade.

Bron and his band of baboons kept flying to a

branch above the action, where they could still see. They were laughing and taking bets on who was going to get eaten.

Nathanial yelled at his knife to grow into a sword. Boss had said it was in Spanish mode, but he couldn't remember the command. The closest he could get was, "Grandé, stupid thing, grandé!"

Mila tripped in front of Nathanial and started crawling hysterically toward a dead end drop-off.

Feeling the salamander's breath on his back, Nathanial dove toward Mila, wrapped one arm around her, pulled her in close to his chest, and threw his other arm up with the battle blade centered in his palm and parallel to the ground. He squinted with determination as he saw the mouth of the salamander opening over his outstretched arm. It was then that the metal of the blade arched over Nathanial's knuckles and expanded outward like two paper folding fans opening up to become a shiny bowed circle. The salamander hit face-first into the newly formed shield and rebounded back from the shocking impact.

"Follow me," Nathanial said to Mila, knowing the salamander's shock would only be momentary.

They got up and jumped to the next tree branch. Nathanial saw that Bron was still holding the backpack as he continued joyfully spectating from above. It gave Nathanial an idea. The salamander was getting its bearings and heading toward the trunk to make another come around.

"Bron, throw me the backpack!" Nathanial yelled up to him commandingly.

Bron's expression hardened immediately at the request. "Why?" he asked coldly.

"Just give it to me!" Nathanial demanded, but he could see it wasn't going to happen from Bron's stern expression.

Nathanial spotted a limb that hung down from Bron's branch.

"Mila, get over to that next branch. I'm going to try something," Nathanial said keeping an eye on the approaching salamander.

Mila seemed uncomfortable leaving Nathanial, but he insisted, and she made the jump.

As hoped, Bron began to fly toward the next over-branch. Nathanial sprinted up the low-hanging limb, jumped when Bron passed over it, and snatched the backpack out of his hands. He turned back, kicked off the branch, and landed on the salamander.

It was slippery, much like trying to stay atop a bucking ice rink, but Nathanial managed to stay on and find what he was looking for in the backpack. He pulled out Bunny's bag of dust and threw a handful of its contents over the salamander. It shrank immediately.

Nathanial cupped his hands quickly over the salamander, scooped it up into his encircling palms, and looked into its little face through the tiny opening between his thumbs. "How's it feel, buddy?" he said with triumph.

Nathanial's momentary exhilaration was squashed by the century kids' glowering expressions that marked him as a dead man. Nathanial let the salamander go free and stuffed Bunny's bag into his pocket.

Mila jumped over to him and whispered, "We need to get inside. Now."

Nathanial stood and casually walked with Mila towards the trunk. The century kids jumped down to block their path.

"How'd you know that was in there, Nat?" Bron asked as he angrily snatched the backpack out of his hand.

Nathanial tried to think quickly, "Because I saw it in there."

Bron grabbed Nathanial's shirt and pulled him up onto his toes. "How did you know what it was?"

Mila cried, "Stop it!" and pushed Bron back.

Kale grabbed her and said, "Oh, no you don't, Skilla. This doesn't concern you."

"Calm down," Nathanial said. "I'm not the human, if that's what you're getting at. Let me go! And you," Nathanial pointed at Kale, "don't touch her."

Bron seemed unsure and Nathanial played off of it. "Seriously, spit," Nathanial pressed on, using the word he'd heard Bron use, "let me explain." Bron let him go and looked to Kale who was loosening his grip on Mila— but still kept a hold of her arm.

"Go ahead," Bron said, "but I'm warning you, don't feed me a bunch of scat. We're a long way's up to be a sprite without wings."

Nathanial tried to act as though the threat of death didn't bother him, and he managed his sudden surge of wooziness. "Come on, haven't you seen a dust bag before? I knew what it was the second I looked in the backpack. I've bought the stuff a couple of times for fun. It makes me think the backpack's not a human's, though."

"It's a human backpack," Sil argued.

"Yeah, I don't mean it's not from a human, just that it's not a human's." They didn't seem to be getting it. "Like none of you have ever stolen a human thing before?" Nathanial shrugged. "Some sprite probably thought it was tap, shrank it, and took it for himself."

"Why was it all the way down here then?" Jax

asked with a lifted brow.

"They must have dropped it!" Nathanial laughed.

Bron leaned in sternly and asked, "Why so interested in looking at its contents when we found it?"

Nathanial faltered then quickly put his smirk back on, "Come on. You guys looked so excited. I wanted to see if I could help figure out who's it was. Sorry, but I don't think it's a human's."

Bron stared at him. Nathanial didn't think they were buying it, but he couldn't give himself away. There didn't appear to be anything in the backpack to link him to it, and so he held Bron's gaze.

"Fine," Bron said.

"What?" Kale blurted out still holding Mila. "You don't seriously believe him?"

"Let's go, guys," Bron said spreading his wings. "It's almost dark and I don't feel much like owl-spotting tonight."

Sil and Jax followed Bron in flight. Kale turned Mila toward himself and said, "Don't think I'm so easily convinced." He shook her. "I know you were following us and I know what you're trying to do. If Nat's not the human, then you'll be looking for the real one. If you hinder our plans in any way, I'll come for you myself." He pushed her away and took flight.

Mila turned to Nathanial and asked, "What do you think you're doing?"

Nathanial shook his head, taken aback by her anger. He'd expected her to be as relieved as he was that his charade had worked. He'd never had to lie to get out of trouble before, and he'd been very surprised at how good he'd been at it.

Mila walked closer to him. "I could see it in your eyes," she whispered. "Do you realize the mess you're in? Why would a human wish to be a sprite?"

It was like she was reading his mind. He knew she knew, and he didn't feel any point in denying it. "I don't know," he said honestly.

She tilted her head.

"I mean it," Nathanial said. "I can't remember. I wish I could because I think I'm supposed to be doing something important, but my memories are all jumbled up."

Mila sighed, seeming to have accepted this as the truth. She took one of the half dozen necklaces from around her neck. It was thick-chained with a heavy metal amulet that had several metallic colored circles all looping around each other within its strong frame.

"The century sprites will be looking closely at

you, now that they suspect you, and this necklace will make it difficult for them to see you as anything other than a sprite. Also, you need to know why you've done this to yourself." Mila turned the necklace and put it around Nathanial's neck.

Her eyes dilated as she looked into his and she asked, "Why would you wish to be a sprite?"

Sounds and images flooded Nathanial's mind. He was on a pirate ship, the *Argosy*. The girl with the kind, dark eyes and a splash of freckles, Aliya, turned toward him and warned him not to trust sprites. Then it was raining on the boat and he grabbed her hand. They were being chased by a massive sprite; his name, Nathanial instantly recalled, was Cyron. A troll of a sprite, colored the same as the open sea, with dark splotches running across his sharp cheekbones. He was her keeper and he had trapped Aliya on that boat for three years without her knowledge. Nathanial was the one who had to tell her, "*You were trapped in a time loop. The* Argosy *sailed through the Bermuda Triangle every day and returned to port without you ever knowing it had left.*" She was devastated.

Then Nathanial remembered fire. It was surrounding Aliya and him as they rode a dragonfly-like beast, an Odonata. Aliya caught Nathanial when he fell off the speeding animal.

A flash forward and Nathanial saw Cyron take roughly hold of Aliya. Nathanial was reaching to pull her free, but Cyron pushed him coldly to the ground. Aliya was screaming.

Then they were in a waiting room. Each of them would be getting a wish-exchange hearing, set up to decide whether or not they'd be returned to factory status, resuming a life of service to the sprites. Aliya was crying. With Cyron there to speak against her, she felt her case was doomed. Nathanial told her not to worry and that if she were sent back to the *Argosy*, he would just have to go rescue her again.

"Only a sprite can find the *Argosy*," Aliya had said, and so they made a plan. Nathanial would exchange his wish for one that would change sprite law. No longer would humans be used for sprite gain without first granting permission and receiving some sort of compensation for being used as factories. With this change, they could both be free.

From behind a crowd of observing sprites, Nathanial watched helplessly as Aliya's hearing went horribly wrong. Her wish sprite revealed that an ancient blood curse on Aliya's maternal line had been activated and would kill her if she did not return to the *Argosy*. Doing what she thought necessary to save Aliya, the wish sprite granted Cyron custody and permission to take Aliya back to the prison from which Nathanial had just helped her to escape.

Nathanial dwelled on some of the words that the wish sprite had spoken during the hearing. *"A blood curse can only be drawn out by the one who put it there."* He had been determined to find that sprite and demand the curse be removed.

He then recalled his own hearing. He requested the wish exchange that would alter sprite law, but Phlegm, Mr. P, shook his head and said, "Humans have no authority to change sprite law." Nathanial remembered how he felt he was losing everything, how he had seemed to have no control or rights in this sprite world; how could he ever help Aliya if he couldn't even help himself? Phlegm drove the problem home by stressing, "Only a sprite can change sprite law." That's when Nathanial had shouted, "Then I wish to be a sprite!"

Nathanial shook the images clear from his vision. Mila did the same. Nathanial knew she had seen his memories. Her eyes dazzled with the same realization as his. They held each other's gaze.

Nathanial said, "I have to go get her."

At the same time Mila said, "You did it for her."

Nathanial thought for a minute and said, "Will

you help me?"

Mila looked surprised and unsure. "Why do you think I can help?"

"Because I've only been a sprite for a day and you've been one—*always*. And because Kale said you'd be looking for the human and not to get in their way. Doesn't that mean you were looking to help the human?" He thought about that. "But maybe that makes its wrong of me to ask for your help. I don't want to get you into any trouble."

Mila bit her lip. "I'm just going to say what I'm thinking here, and we'll see where that leads. The rumors of you are everywhere. Sprites can't believe the council would allow a factory to try being a sprite. Even the progressive sprites, who once *literally* fought for human rights, see this as opening up old wounds, and they don't want a fourth rebellion.

"Bron would give anything to find out who this rumored factory sprite is. He wants to impress the Swartza, who've hated the council ever since elections began replacing their century families with commoners. Bron is from one of those fallen-from-grace families, and he hopes to prove himself worthy of Swartza acceptance. They would likely reward him for bringing you to them. Imagining himself exposing the council's concealment of you is probably what gets him through most of Mr. P's classes." She scoffed. "We can be sure he'll be keeping an eye on you, but the necklace should cover your butt if you play it right. He won't believe a human capable of what it can help you do. Still, I'm not sure we should chance sticking around Hyperion."

Nathanial fiddled with the metal around his neck and kept a pleading expression on his face.

"As for Kale," she continued with a roll of her eyes, "his people have always had it out for my kind, so his threat means nothing to me. They hate humans, and my people have made our stance against haters clear.

"Should I abandon my training at Hyperion for some changeling I just met?" Mila wavered. "That is the real question. You seem like a good guy, brave even, but too impulsive. You don't think things through before you act." She looked him up and down. "Still, you kind of saved my life just now."

Nathanial was hopeful. Her out-loud thinking seemed to be leaning in his favor.

"If we do this, we have to do it fast, but smart," she said nodding. "We can't give Bron the chance to figure out who you are. We'll have to stay under the radar when out on the streets, too. We might have to do some pretty shady things. Are you sure you're up to it?"

"It's the whole reason I'm here," Nathanial said with a sense of purpose flooding him with anticipation. This realization was a churning soup in his stomach. He couldn't believe that no one had told him. Not Bunny, not Phlegm, and not Boss. He had straight-up asked Boss about Aliya and he had called her *just a girl*. Nathanial was angry to think about it. How could they just leave her with Cyron— another year of her life to be stolen aboard that ship? It was unthinkable. He had to do something.

"Just tell me what to do and we'll do it," Nathanial said, his excitement racing.

"Well, we can't head out in the dark," Mila said, regarding the deep purples in the sky. "And I'm going to need some supplies. Try to get some sleep, pack light, and meet me in the cafeteria at sunrise."

The flood of memories and the prospect of taking action had pumped him full of adrenaline. He was ready to go and wanted to argue that they do so immediately, but he managed to bite his tongue. To disagree with the guide he had just recruited wouldn't do him any favors. He nodded and reached to take off the necklace.

"No," Mila said pressing it back down onto his

chest, "like I said, you need to keep it. But under your shirt."

Nathanial dipped the necklace into his shirt. Having to hide it meant he was adding another secret to his already complicated life. "Okaaay, but why?"

"It's a tap-aid. My father makes them. But they're underground."

"Meaning it's illegal?"

"Only because the sprites in power want to keep them for themselves—to give them an advantage over the general public." She shook her head in disgust.

"Because it lets you read minds?"

Mila smirked. "No—well, yes. If you are a Skilla, it enhances that ability, but, in general, they open up your tap. It speeds up your connectivity." Nathanial remained quizzical. "Ok, so, like, you were trying to get your shield to open earlier, right? But it only worked in a moment of desperation."

Nathanial nodded.

"Yeah, try again," she said with a sideways grin.

Nathanial looked at the battle blade which was still in its shield form and thought *sword*. It instantaneously swished up into a sword. Nathanial jumped back and gasped in astonishment.

"Wow..." he said.

"Yeah." Mila nodded, "you might want to keep that weapon hidden, too. Those century goats probably thought it was just a pop shield, but it looks like a lot more than that. So, I'll see you in the morning."

She turned and Nathanial said, "Hey! Thanks."

Mila eyeballed him up and down. Through a slanted smile she said, "Don't thank me yet, changeling. I'm not promising your survival here." And she jumped to the next branch.

Nathanial stared after her. His sword shrank back down into its knife size.

Chapter Ten

FACTORY SAFETY

*N*athanial couldn't sleep. There were way too many thoughts spinning around in his head. He remembered everything from the previous year now, and he just wanted to reach Aliya. He had made a promise and he was not going to break it. He couldn't believe all the trivial things he had worried about at regular school: if his classmates accepted him, how he'd disappoint his teachers and mom if he didn't make straight As, how Brad would make fun of him if he didn't wear the right outfit. All these stupid little things, while Aliya was being tortured on a ship by a vicious sea sprite—a Nixie, and all because his memory had been stolen to try and make him a factory again… all for sprite gain. He was disgusted.

It made him think about Bunny and everything she had done for him last year: the battle blade, keeping him in disguise through all his adventures, and always answering his questions like there was nothing she wanted to hide from him in the world. He felt a guilty twist in his stomach for thinking she was just a wild thing that kind of annoyed him when she had pushed him through the Niche in his bedroom.

He wished he could apologize. He wished he could hug her and thank her. But really, he wished she had told him about Aliya. Maybe she thought Boss would tell him. But of course Boss wouldn't. He always had a way of manipulating Nathanial, since the very beginning. It was clear now why he didn't trust Boss and always seemed to want to snap at him—something he'd never do to a real teacher. The same went for Phlegm. Both of them had worked on Nathanial for years, keeping him sick and stuck in his bedroom, and when his wish to be well had finally been granted, they'd sought to take it away from him.

At least Boss had seemed to come around a bit, more than Phlegm anyway. He'd even represented Aliya at her hearing—but he had failed hadn't he— and now he wouldn't even speak of her. The anger balled up in Nathanial's throat and he tossed and turned with these bitter thoughts for hours.

As the lazy morning sun peeked between the treetops, Nathanial got dressed, packed some essentials in a bag, and headed out the door. He was the only student in the cafeteria when he entered; the breakfast foods were just being set out at their stations. His anxiety was keeping him from feeling his hunger, but since Mila wasn't there yet, and he knew it might be a while until they ate, he went over to get the Hyperion Breakfast Special.

A golf cart–sized orange had replaced the honeysuckles at the drink dispenser, and Nathanial filled up a glass of fresh juice.

Nathanial took a seat and absentmindedly scarfed down the scramble of chopped beans, eggs, and potatoes. There was an unidentifiable white and chewy substance in the mix but his preoccupation on the cafeteria entrance kept him from worrying about it too much.

"Wow, I didn't expect to see you here so early!" came a cheerful voice from behind Nathanial. He choked on his mouthful of food and sent little white specks across the table. He turned his head to see a smiley Spassel with a tray of food. Spassel came around and sat down in front of Nathanial. "You really took to heart my advice yesterday."

Nathanial's quizzical expression made it clear he had no idea what advice Spassel was referring to.

"Early is on time, on time is late," Spassel courteously reminded him.

Nathanial took a big gulp of juice and nodded.

That's when Mila entered the cafeteria. Nathanial

watched her go over to the bread booth and stuff some rolls into a rucksack.

"Ah, well, sorry to ditch you like this, Spassel, but I need to grab my school jacket from my room," Nathanial said getting up from the table.

"Oh," Spassel said, "but you don't have to go right now. We have plenty of time before class starts, and I need to show you how to get there. Remember we have a different rotation today. I can go with you to your room if you like, before class. Have a pastry!" Spassel held up one of the cream-filled breads from his tray.

Mila made eye contact with Nathanial. She immediately knew the dilemma. She walked over to Nathanial and said, "Hey Nat. Would you mind helping me out with something?"

"Oh," Nathanial said raising his brows. "Sure. I'll catch you later, Spassel."

Spassel watched the two of them as they left the cafeteria. Mila wasn't wearing her school uniform; this only added to Spassel's curiosity and suspicion. Instead she wore a black leather jacket and a purple vest with a pair of casual jeans and high boots.

"We'd better hurry," Mila said as soon as they were out of Spassel's sight.

Nathanial briskly followed Mila down a narrow hall until she suddenly stopped.

"I'm getting an A-vibe," she said as she knelt down to pull her tablet out of her rucksack. She placed it on the ground and put her hand on the screen. "That's dreg," she said with a sigh. She sounded like she was responding to a conversation, but Nathanial couldn't hear or see anyone. He gathered it was a sprite phone call. "How long then?" she continued. "Uh-huh. Well I don't know…You know how they can block my kind. We'll just have to hope. Let me know as soon as you have them."

Mila put the tablet back in her rucksack and stood up with a look of disappointment. "We can't go just yet."

"What? Why?" Nathanial gawped.

"My guy couldn't get your fake papers as quick as we'd hoped. He needs more time, maybe another day or two."

"Papers?"

"For Niche hopping. It's the best way to find your friend."

"Well I can't stay here. What about the century kids?" Nathanial gulped. "They're bound to find out about me."

"Just keep up the act. You did great last night. You almost had *me* fooled—and you didn't even have the necklace on yet. Those slags are more bulk than brains anyway. Call them century kids because that's how slow they are." She chuckled.

Nathanial stood with his mouth ajar. Just the night before she had said they would need to move fast. Now she was acting like it wouldn't hurt to wait. He was sure Bron was going to have his head.

"Hey, you two." It was Spassel, smiling his way toward them from down the hall. "Thought I should tag along. Nat really needs me to show him to today's rotation. He's been put into the same classes as me since it was too late in the term for him to pick his own. I'd hate for us not to be able to find each other. He doesn't have a tablet to contact me, after all. I can also help you with whatever you need, Mila!"

Mila shook her head and said, "It's all good, Spaz. I'll see you second period." She turned down the hall without giving Nathanial another glance.

"Whelp. It's just you and me then, buddy." Spassel beamed at Nathanial. "Should we go get your jacket?"

The first class of the day was called Factory Safety. It was an elective that Bron and his gang were not taking, much to Nathanial's relief. Mila wasn't there either. In fact, there were only ten sprites in the odd room. It wasn't so much the room that was odd as what was in it. Giant replicas of human body parts were scattered throughout the high-ceilinged space.

The class was gathered before an armless upper body that was the size of a house. Its polo-shirted chest sat on the wooden floor, giving it the appearance of a man who'd wandered into some quicksand. The expression on its face did not reflect this sentiment as it smiled goofily out into space.

"Everyone, get into a belt and harness," Mr. Quick, the amber-colored teacher, said, already sporting the gear himself. "We're going to practice wax retrieval today."

Nathanial picked up one of the heavy belts and examined its contents. In individual slots and pouches he found a feather, a *web-o-matic* pistol, a grappling hook, a syringe, several empty vials, and a multi-use tool with scissors, a knife, and pincers. There were also some worn rubbery gloves, like the ones that had helped him grip the obstacles in P.E. He put them on.

Clipping the belt around his waist, Nathanial looked up to the man-shaped boulder before him and tried to make the best out of what he was about to attempt. "Well, you've always wanted to try rock climbing," he reminded himself.

There were a few student helpers assisting the class with putting their climbing harnesses on. They would be acting as belayers, holding the safety ropes and ready to catch any student should they fall.

Nathanial watched Spassel, who was getting a good tug on his rope by a cute budding-pink sprite. Spassel momentarily seemed to be getting his own colors, but it wasn't yellow that was glowing through his hot cheeks. Nathanial couldn't help but laugh at the innocent gawking expression on Spassel's face. He received an excited thumbs-up when Spassel caught him looking.

Nathanial's student helper was a tall rust-tinted fellow that made Nathanial's harness so tight his ankle-length pants were soon knee-high with fabric stuffed up into places where not even a proper wedgie could find room to hide.

"For the winged and geckites, cranial factory work is breezier than a ride up a shoot," Mr. Quick said, walking before the class. "For the rest of us, it takes practice. The student helpers here today are either flyers or geckites."

Nathanial looked to his helper who winked and held up his hands with wiggling fingers. The fleshy fingers and palms looked natural while un-flexed, but with movement they revealed waves much like the ones on Nathanial's rubber gloves. He assumed his student helper was a geckite.

"Sprites call me Rusty," he introduced himself.

"I'm Nat," Nathanial replied.

"Today is the last day we'll have you in harnesses, so I brought your helpers in for you to get acquainted. They'll be acting as your lifeline after today instead of the rope."

Ugh, so he'd already missed the week of harness training and soon his life would be in the gecko hands of Rusty the wedgie-maker. Great. Spassel couldn't have looked more pleased with the news and gave Nathanial another thumbs-up.

"You might notice this factory replica is larger than life, to prevent us from having to use dust, but if you were to ever be on wax duty, you would be provided with the dust daily. Most everyone knows that natural dust from dust sprites operates instinctively to make that which is small, big and vice versa, all sizes being relative to the sprites which, let's face it, are small. If a sprite needs to be smaller than we naturally are, it takes a controlled amount of modified dust to not shrink us to the point of being dust particles ourselves. There's an elective class specific to the subject if anyone is interested in becoming a dust chemist. All right, enough chatter, let's get to it," Mr. Quick said with a clap of his hands. "The student to bring me their fully filled vials first gets to dip into my bag of brand-new gear!"

"Let's do this!" Nathanial's helper said while slapping him on the back. He pulled the rope until Nathanial was dangling painfully on his tippy-toes.

Never having attempted such a feat as climbing a human torso before—or even coming close to dreaming about it—Nathanial was lost on what his first move should be. He surveyed the sprites around him. They were pulling themselves skyward in great bounds, grasping at the polo shirt for each advancing lift.

"Come on, iceberg, get moving," were his helper's motivational words.

Nathanial remembered the sprite P.E. class from the day before and thought he'd be okay using his arm strength like the rest of the class. He took a handful of blue shirt and pulled. The lift was a success. He flew three body lengths upward, but his exhilaration at this accomplishment proved to be premature. Nathanial had accidentally pushed out as he'd pulled up, leaving him unable to grasp the shirt again. He screamed, kicked, and flailed during a few seconds of falling before his helper pulled the rope taut.

"Ok," Rusty said lowering Nathanial to touch back down. "Let's try that again, but this time keep your elbows out and your back straight. Doesn't hurt to point your toes either."

Nathanial embarrassedly turned back to the model human, sighed, and looked to all the sprites that'd already made it to the collarbone. Even Spassel was up with the rest of them. That was until his pretty pink helper said, "You're doing great, Spassel," and his foot slipped. It became apparent in that moment how diagonal Spassel's ascent had been. When he fell, his rope arced across the torso and tripped all the sprites in its path, which happened to be *all* of the sprites.

"Looks like you still have a chance at that prize," Rusty said with an encouraging nudge while the class rained down around them.

Keeping his elbows out and his entire body straight, Nathanial lifted again and easily grabbed ahold of the shirt at the apex of his rise. He felt somewhat guilty at his advantage, seeing as how most the class was still busy untangling their ropes, but it did make for a much less daunting task without a bunch of sprites jumping over his head. He was climbing up onto the shoulder, by the time the class started toward him, and he was feeling proud until he looked at the large ear canal above him and realized he had no idea how to collect the wax.

Searching the supplies belted around his waist, Nathanial picked out the multi-tool and the syringe. With a single jump, he was into the yellow cavernous space of the ear and his feet squished into the smelly mushy flooring.

"Ew....You gotta be kidding me," Nathanial said in full realization of what he was trying to do.

He took an empty vial from his belt, squatted down, and looked at the two options he held for the task. "I can't believe I'm doing this." He sniggered and attempted to suck some earwax up into the syringe.

It was working, but very slowly. The needle was too thin and the earwax too thick. He could already hear classmates just outside of the ear. It wouldn't be long before he had much more experienced company around him and his advantage would be lost.

Nathanial squirted the syringe contents into the vial, only filling it halfway. Someone was in the ear entrance. It was time to get down and dirty. He plunged the entire vial into a clump of earwax and pressed it down to the floor until the clear glass was full. Doing it this way put him elbow-deep into the stench-ridden goop, but he had all seven vials filled in less than a minute. When he turned around, he saw half the class staring at him with syringes in their hands.

"Oh," he said noticing one important detail. "You took the needle off. Guess that helps."

Then he passed through the group who quickly dispersed from his path as not to be touched by his filthy arms.

Standing on the shoulder, looking down at his helper, Nathanial yelled, "So I'm ready to come down now. Should I just jump and repel down this thing or what?"

"Yeah!" Rusty called back. "Lean back and walk it down. I'll show you a quicker way next time you're not on a rope."

Nathanial had watched plenty of documentaries on climbing and repelling, and it'd always been the repel that looked like the most fun. He was told to walk it down, but Nathanial wanted to try something else. He leaned back, took a couple of steps, then started jumping. When Rusty got the gist of what Nathanial was trying to do, he let the rope out a few feet at a time so Nathanial could fall a ways before coming back toward the torso to jump again. It was the most fun Nathanial had had in a while. So much so that he was laughing when he touched down.

"All right, spit!" Rusty exclaimed, impressed. "Give me some-a-diss!" And he raised his hand as if asking for a high five, but then noticed Nathanial's ear-waxed arms. "On second thought…" he put his hand back down.

"Haven't seen someone plunge it in years." Mr. Quick laughed on approach to Nathanial and tossed him a towel.

Nathanial wiped his arms off, but the smell remained. "I can smell why," Nathanial said, scrunching his nose.

"Well, you've definitely earned this," Mr. Quick said and opened a black bag just enough for one of Nathanial's arms to fit. "Take one surprise item from the bag."

Nathanial smiled excitedly and stuck his arm deep in the bag. Everything seemed to be wrapped up, so he couldn't make out what anything was by touch. He took hold of something and pulled it out. The wrapper said, *Geck-a-grip Glove Pro, for all your gripping needs.* He pulled it off and found brand-new rubber gloves with gecko-foot-like waves on the palm.

"Wow, thanks!" Nathanial said, slipping off the class-provided gloves so he could put on the new ones. They were ten times more comfortable than the old ones, and formed perfectly to his hands. "They feel great!"

"They're the best geck-gloves on the market," Mr. Quick said, smiling. "You won't slip off any surface with those babies on."

The rest of the class disappointedly started to join together around him and the teacher.

"Don't worry, class. You'll all get another chance next time," Mr. Quick said, closing up the bag.

Spassel was the last to join the group, and it looked as though he'd taken a dive into an earwax pool.

"Whoa, Spaz, what happened to you?" Nathanial asked the somber mucky face.

"My foot got stuck in a wax pot." Spassel pouted.

"Both of you are excused," Mr. Quick said plugging his nose. "Go shower."

Chapter Eleven

A Growing Problem

Spassel hadn't stopped talking about the student helper he'd had in Factory Safety class, even when he had to raise his voice for Nathanial to hear from the next shower stall, and he continued to do so as they walked, damp-headed and smelling of fresh sap, down the hall toward their next class.

"Flori," he said for the hundredth time. "She is something."

"Yeah, I know," Nathanial said, shaking his head.

"I never thought much on flying, but now I'm thinking wings might not be so bad after all."

"So it is possible to *choose* to grow them?" Nathanial asked, interested in that prospect.

"It's possible, but one of the most difficult and painful things to do if it's not in your blood. Then there's all the upkeep. You have to get your clothing tailored and everything. I only know one sprite not born to it that's succeeded."

Nathanial groaned at the unlikelihood. "Sure

would make things easier, though. Factory Safety class, just for instance. Zip right up to the top of that torso, no problem. By the way, why were there only ten sprites taking that class? I'd think it'd be a requirement, given that's what most sprites do for a living."

"I know what you mean." Spassel nodded. "Most of the population works on human factories, yet it's still considered an undesirable middle-class job. If it weren't for all those workers though, the high-class couldn't survive. I guess most people come here to try for something better than factory work. Otherwise, you could just stay home and shadow your parents."

"Then why did you pick it for your elective?"

"It's my backup. In case my big-shot dream job doesn't work out. Which, face it, how often do sprites get their dream jobs? I'll probably be a factory worker in the end, and I want to be safe when that happens."

"So, what's your dream job?" Nathanial asked with a smile.

Spassel looked sideways at him. "I don't want to tell."

"Oh, come on!" Nathanial goaded. "You can tell me."

"We're here," Spassel said, quickening his steps

and walking out onto a branch.

The branch that Nathanial followed Spassel onto was more like a garden out of *Alice's Adventures in Wonderland* than another part of the tree. The grass was cut short along the paths, but towered around the outer edges. Flowers arced over the open space, creating colorful shadows, and mushrooms were hollowed out to form gazebos. It was one of those moments that reminded Nathanial how very small he really was.

The class was gathered in a central mushroom gazebo. Nathanial immediately spotted Bron leaning against one of the entrance posts. Nathanial gulped. Moment of truth: Would Bron pounce or had Nathanial's charade been enough to keep his human-ness in question? Bron made eye contact. Nathanial nodded, thinking it was best to act not guilty. Bron nodded in return—a good sign.

"What's up, Bron?" Nathanial asked smoothly.

"Just waiting for my girlfriend to arrive." Bron smirked at his buddies.

Nathanial glanced over at Sil and Jax who were bumping elbows, and then to Kale who would probably give him that analytical expression no matter how good of an actor Nathanial turned out to be.

Nathanial cleared his throat and smiled back

over to Bron. "Who's your girlfriend?"

"Ms. Kaysea, the finest nectar sprite I've ever laid eyes on. She smells so sweet my lungs turn to sugar just being around her," Bron said, being more poetic than Nathanial thought possible.

"Wow, our teacher's a nectar sprite. Can't wait to meet her," Nathanial said, smirking with his recovered memory of Mr. P, when he knew him as Phlegm, stating his intentions to marry a nectar sprite one day.

"You can meet her all you want, but she's mine, got it!" Bron said getting in his face.

That was more like what Nathanial had expected. "Hey, she's all yours, Bron!" Nathanial laughed as he put up his hands and backed away.

The scent of honeysuckles wafted over Nathanial and the expressions of all the tough boys in front of him went slack. Nathanial turned around to the sight of sugar and spice and everything nice personified into a golden sprite goddess. No wonder Bron had a schoolboy crush. She was Marilyn Monroe dipped in honey!

"Good day, class," her bell voice sang on approach.

"Good day," the class responded in unison, Bron loudest of all, stepping forward and straightening up.

"We're going to continue the basics of Nature Tuning with a little grass growing today, if everyone would follow me please," she said, swishing her flowing amber locks and sending a fresh breeze of sweetness toward the class.

It was a little funny to watch Bron stumble over himself—and others—as he hurried to be directly behind Ms. Kaysea. It was the only class in which he insisted on being in the front, and everyone kept clear to allow it.

The group stopped in a clearing where a tuft of grass sprouted an inch above the freshly cut turf that was all around them. Ms. Kaysea turned to the class and said, "Jay, could you step forward, please."

A boy with chocolate-colored poofy hair stepped through the crowd and stopped in front of the teacher.

"You're the only one here with the green thumb blood trait. Would you mind being the first to attempt assisting this patch?" Ms. Kaysea asked gently.

Nathanial furrowed his brow at this. How could Ms. Kaysea know what his blood trait was? Without color, how could anyone tell any difference? Maybe it was on school records, he guessed.

"Adults can tell," a voice came in a sudden

whisper from behind Nathanial.

Nathanial jumped and turned with surprise to see Mila. He had thought no one was behind him.

"Jeez, you trying to scare the pants off me?" he said catching his skipping heart. Then he realized what she had said, "Wait, were you reading my mind again?"

"It's a little hard not to," she said lifting a brow. "Most sprites have a natural guard against it. I'm lucky if direct skin contact works with them, but you're not like that. Your thoughts spread through the ground you walk on." She smirked with a slow wave toward their feet.

Nathanial gulped and thought he needed to find a way to change that. He didn't like the idea of anyone reading his mind.

"Aw." Mila pouted. "You're already building blocks. Well, that's probably for the best. Not all Skilla are as cool as I am."

"So, you can't read my mind now?"

"Not if you don't want me to."

Nathanial nodded with relief. "Good. That's a little freaky."

Mila shrugged.

"But you were saying adults can tell what kind of sprite a kid is?" Nathanial picked back up.

"Yeah, it's so they can help their own, you know.

Like, if a sprite kid gets orphaned, they can be helped by the appropriate surrogates. It's an old evolutionary hangover."

"Interesting," Nathanial said wondering what adults saw when they looked at him.

Just then there was a yelp from the front of the class. Jay's shirt was caught on the tip of a towering blade of grass that he'd made grow too fast. The shirt ripped and he slipped screaming down the blade like it was a steep slide. When he hit the ground, the breath was knocked out of him and his arm was bleeding from the worst kind of paper cut: one not made by paper.

"Shay!" Ms. Kaysea called to a student helper nearby, "bring me the bamboo and adhesive!"

The student helper rushed over with a little box. Nathanial kept getting closer and closer to the action. Something looked off about that cut.

Shay pulled a pack of leaves from the box and wiped Jay's *white* blood away. Nathanial widened his eyes. Sprites did not bleed like humans! Nathanial absentmindedly put a hand to the cut he'd received from the Hyperion glider escapade, even though his long-sleeved uniform was hiding it. Ms. Kaysea wrapped a bamboo leaf around the kid's cut and slathered it with clear goop from a jar.

"It's ok, class," Ms. Kaysea assured everyone as she helped Jay to his feet. "Here is an example of Nature Tuning at its best. By using natural remedies, we tap into our plant and animal kinship, thereby quickening the healing process. When we are close to the trees, and the grass, to fresh rivers and the open air, that is when we feel our best. It is when we are at our strongest."

Nathanial thought everything she was saying was nice and all, but he was currently preoccupied with the white blood that had come from Jay's cut. He had cut himself just yesterday and the blood was red. What if Bron had seen that! Was that truly why Boss had given him the hoodie, not for concern of the cold, but to hide his red scrapes? Oh, he was going to have a talk with Boss when he got down to see him later. The secrets were not acceptable anymore. They could get him killed!

The rest of the class was spent on Ms. Kaysea explaining the theory behind helping grass grow. Nathanial supposed the accident had deterred her from further hands-on attempts. Anger and anxiety toward Boss kept Nathanial from being able to pay too much attention to what was being said. He wanted to confront Boss about having his memories back and wanting to go after Aliya, but he knew it was the wrong move. Boss hadn't told Nathanial about her exactly because he knew Nathanial would want to go after her. So he wouldn't let him know he had his memories back just yet. But maybe he could at least ask him why he didn't warn him about the blood.

Before he realized it, the class was over. Spassel was headed toward him when Bron moved in, which sent Spassel on a quick retreat.

"What'd I tell ya?" Bron said punching Nathanial's arm. "Perfect, isn't she?"

"Yeah," Nathanial nodded. "Got yourself a keeper there."

Bron laughed. "Are you ready for the second best class of the semester? This one being the first, because of my girlfriend, of course."

"Of course," Nathanial placated. "I'm ready. What is it?"

"Oh, you'll see my friend, you'll see."

Chapter Twelve

TRICKS IN TREES

*A*t lunch, Nathanial was forced to sit and listen to Bron do nothing but harp on about Ms. Kaysea and refuse to tell Nathanial anything about their next class. When Nathanial saw Ms. Kaysea enter the lunchroom, he took a passive victory by withholding the knowledge of her presence from Bron, then he had a little surprise when he saw who she'd come to see. Ms. Kaysea glided over to Mr. P who was alone in a corner booth. She gave a little golden glass vial to him. Mr. P turned bright red and quickly rose to his feet, bowing and bumping food off of his plate in the process.

Nathanial smirked. Was that nectar she was giving him? It looked like Bron had some competition.

Not soon enough, lunch was over and Nathanial found himself and his twenty-odd classmates within a small domed room covered in sparking blue veined structures. An eerily fluorescent yellow light emanated upon the sprites' pale skin, similar to standing beneath a black light. The teacher, Mr. Bones, appeared freakish from this effect. His teeth and eyes reflected bright yellow and his skin a radioactive green. His thick hair was like twisted straw upon his shoulders. His bright teeth smiled out at them

"Good afternoon, class, and thank you for joining me for another dive into the precision of will that we all like to call the tap. We will continue this week to bring vibrations into tap before we move on to the actual tricks that the tap is most used for."

Nathanial pondered this intro. It sounded as though tapping was like the next step to catching vibrations. He remembered Spassel's rant about it at lunch the day before. The tap allowed the sprites to see vibrations. He perked his ears up, wondering why everyone seemed to make such a big fuss about this.

"If you wanted to put a trick in this tree to have it lean left, for instance," Mr. Bones said. He walked over to one of the veins in the wall and pointed at it. "Just feeling for a vibration might not give your trick the strength required for the desired effect. You need to physically grab the vibration to perform the trick, and for that you need the visual tap. This particular vein would be nearly impossible to find without the tap. But now that you can see it, you can directly place your trick into the reaction center that tells the tree the wind is blowing, even if there is no wind. This can come in handy when you need to get to an adjacent tree and can't quite make the jump. How I know this is the proper vibrational vein is more complicated, but similar to how you know which Niche leads to a city and not to the middle of the woods: It's all about the vibe."

Nathanial felt a twinge in his stomach. He had no idea how to tell where a Niche would take him. He had thought they all just lead to the nearest sprite city or town. How was he supposed to tell the difference between the vibes in a Niche?

"I personally reach out with a command vibe to intensify. See how this vein is glowing brighter than the rest?" Mr. Bones moved his hand across the spot. "I felt for the vibration and moved along it until my proximity closed in on the strongest vibe within the tree. I then commanded it to intensify, therefore bringing out this strong glow. This is how you go beyond vibration and into tap.

"You might think we don't need the tap as we could feel the vibe close enough without it. Indeed, for centuries that is how we went about things, but performing the trick would not be direct without the tap and that leads to weak results.

"Many find their own method of performing tricks with simple vibrations, but for now, let's try to tap it my way and see what you think. Everyone spread around the room and try to brighten this vein by commanding it to do so. It can be found anywhere in the tree. Once you've commanded the vein to glow, please release the vibe and call me over. We are not performing any tricks today."

The tree dimmed as Mr. Bones removed his hand and the students arranged themselves along the wall. Nathanial sighed and found his own patch to stare at. Why this class was one of Bron's favorites, he hadn't quite figured out yet. Bron was currently a few students to his right, having no problem illuminating the vein in front of him. Maybe it was just being good at this class that made him so fond of it.

"I was thinking," a voice came suddenly from his left, "we should try to get to the market." It was Mila.

"Jeez," Nathanial whispered. "How do you sneak up like that?"

Mila shrugged. "You need some real clothes. I saw what you wore after school yesterday. A Hyperion provided get-up will draw attention when it comes time to leave. You got any gold?"

"No," Nathanial said keeping his voice down in fear of their proximity to Bron.

"Ask Boss for some. He's like your guardian here. Shouldn't be a problem."

Nathanial pondered her for a second, thinking how weird it was she knew so much about him because of that memory flash they shared.

"Hey guys, how's it going?" Spassel asked, coming up on Nathanial's other side. "Did you command the vibe yet?"

Nathanial shook his head.

"Hey Spaz, want to come to the market with us?" Mila asked.

"As long as it's after my club meeting," Spassel responded very excitedly.

"You're in a club?" Nathanial asked. "What kind?"

"Ah, you know, role-playing stuff."

"Like Dungeons and Dragons?" Nathanial snickered.

"Never heard of that," Spassel responded with a scrunched nose.

Mr. Bones came up behind the trio. Everyone quickly pretended like they had been trying to catch the vibe. The teacher moved on.

Nathanial wanted to ask Mila when they should go to the market, but found she was gone. Then he turned to ask Spassel where Mila went and instead found Bron.

"Having any luck?" Bron asked with his cronies behind him.

"No, not yet," Nathanial said turning back to the wall.

"You gotta learn how to tap and trick, spit, it's the quickest way to blossom," Bron said, putting his hand on the wall and lighting it up. "Look at that. I'm gifted. Can't wait to cut out of this tree and start ruling the world already." He laughed darkly.

"Really?" Nathanial asked skeptically. "Lighting up a tree to trick it into leaning left is going to put a crown on your head?"

"Seriously, Nat..." Bron's stance turned sharp. "Your vision is narrow if you really think this class is about telling a tree to lean left. It's about the tap, the trick, the control. You learn the little stuff like this and the next step is tricking your enemies into thinking there are a few steps more past the edge of a cliff."

The picture Bron drew was darker than Nathanial had expected. He kept quiet; it was clear Bron wasn't finished.

"This is greater than that old-school vibration-catching Mr. P-thetic spouts on about. Vibrations are weak, but the tap..." He licked his lips and nodded excitedly. "You tap the right vein in something and it has no choice but to bend to your will. Do you get it now, Nat? Why just make something lean when you can make something break?"

Nathanial nodded, trying not to look as freaked out as he felt. "I see."

"Good, now light this beast up!" Bron commanded.

Nathanial put his attention back on the tree and sucked in a boatload of air until his chest couldn't expand any further. Slowly he released the air and closed his eyes. He felt for the tree's vibrations by visualizing what it might look like. He knew it wasn't exactly the way the teacher had described, but the only way he knew how to catch a vibration was from what he'd experienced with Boss and Phlegm. He'd successfully opened a Niche and felt a flying squirrel's heartbeat, both times seeing something light in the dark of his mind. The difference here, it seemed, was to find and command a specific thread within the vibration.

Nathanial could visualize the veins and noted that one of them pulsed brighter and harder than the rest. He felt a strange warmth growing hotter on his chest as he reached out for the thick thread in his mind's eye. He took hold of it, and a glow penetrated the cover of his eyelids. He opened his eyes to the intensity of the room. It traveled from beneath Nathanial's palm and spread out all the way around the domed ceiling like an electrified spiral.

The tree suddenly bent dramatically to the left and everyone in the room tumbled over, accordingly. The heat on his chest felt like a burst of fire and Nathanial grabbed the amulet through his clothes and pulled it away from his singed flesh as he, too, tumbled and landed curled inward over the pain. He would have snatched the necklace off and thrown it across the room if he hadn't remembered it was an illegal item. He just counted to ten and waited hopefully for the amulet to cool.

Maybe Nathanial had knelt for too long because, when he got to his feet, everyone in the room was staring at him.

Mr. Bones walked forward and stopped in front of Nathanial. Nathanial tried to swallow, but his throat was currently stranded in a desert of guilt. Had Mr. Bones seen Nathanial reach for the amulet? Was he about to get kicked out of Hyperion on his second day?

"I've never seen a room light up like that before," Mr. Bones finally said. "But I didn't want you to trick the tree just yet. I always move the class to a different tree for that."

Nathanial gulped. He didn't mean to move the tree. He'd just been thinking of the teacher's lesson and bending the tree had been part of it. Oh, no, all the sprites in all the rooms throughout the school, the cafeteria! Had he hurt anyone?

"Luckily, the school is equipped to handle windy days or I might be worried right now. As it is, I have to say, congratulations."

Nathanial's fear switched gears to confusion.

"I think I've just found my new student helper," Mr. Bones finished with a grin.

The other students closed in around Nathanial with chatters and smiles. They all patted him on the back with words of admiration. It took Nathanial a moment to smile back and nod with thanks to each beaming face that complimented him. The shock of the event hadn't quite evaporated when he caught Mila's eyes. He felt the intensity she conveyed from behind the crowd. This confirmed his suspicions. The amulet had been the cause of the strength behind that trick, and if anyone found out about it, they'd both be expelled. Even though it was nice to have positive attention, Nathanial felt compelled to return the amulet. Having it was just too much of a risk.

In the hall after the class, it took Nathanial a minute to shake off the followers from Tap and Trick Training. Bron didn't want to seem like a groupie, so he was one of the first to leave after a quick "congratulations" and "see you later," but the rest just kept asking over and over how he'd grasped the vibe so powerfully.

Finally, he got to his room and had to close the door on the last handful of sprites, giving them the excuse of lots of homework to do. He went to his desk and sat on the stool. *Don't call any attention to yourself.* Hadn't those been Boss's words? Yeah, that wasn't going real well.

He unbuttoned his shirt and examined the skin under the amulet. There were red swirls in a pattern mimicking that of the amulet, but it didn't look as bad as it had felt.

Nathanial swiped his desk to reveal the Hyperion Portal. It would do him some good to hear his mom's voice right now. It had felt like forever since he'd seen her, even a different lifetime.

The small cleverly designed symbol with the *A* tips touching those of the *V* blinked in the top right corner. Nathanial tapped it and a hand outline appeared on the screen with the words *Audio Vibration Network Activated* in the center. Placing his hand on the outline, he thought of his home phone number, expecting nothing to happen.

It was odd when he heard the ringing in his ears and finally, "Hello."

"Mom," he said with trepidation.

"Nathanial, baby, it's so good to hear your voice. How are you doing out there?"

Sweet relief washed over Nathanial. Hearing the voice of the one who loved and cared for him most, was enough to relieve him of stress. His mom had been his savior through the years of illness and many accompanied depressions. Any time he had felt like giving in to the darkness of unrelenting solitude, she would be there to encourage him and strengthen him. Many of the books he'd read on overcoming insurmountable odds had been given to him by her. He tried to think quickly through all the things he wanted to say about all the things he had seen and the strange choices he'd found he'd made. He wanted her advice on how to proceed. But he had to keep up a roadblock of secrecy. He'd never hid a thing from his mother before. He'd never had a problem talking with her before. But now…

"I'm doing good," he said and paused with the sad realization of his predicament. "How are you?"

"I miss you like crazy," she said. "I want to hear all about your new school. It says here in the pamphlet you'll be learning cultural meditation practices, botany, and zoology!"

Nathanial laughed at the human terminology that slightly represented his current classes, but didn't quite express the truth of it. "Yeah, I'm learning lots about all that stuff. It's pretty neat."

"Good, good. I'm so glad to hear that."

There was a moment of silence. Nathanial considered his plan to go after Aliya. He wondered if he should make up some excuse, in case she didn't hear back from him for a while, but there was no way to know when he'd be leaving or for how long. Maybe he could call her again along the way. He probably shouldn't say anything. He didn't want to worry her.

"How do you like Mr. Bozeman?" Suzy asked.

"Who?"

"Mr. Bozeman, your mentor!" Suzy reminded with surprise.

"Oh, yeah, of course," Nathanial said, remembering Boss's human persona. "You just cut out for a second there, um, yeah he's alright." Nathanial was still trying to figure out what he really thought of Boss.

"I could tell you didn't trust him at the house," Suzy said. "I really think he just wants the best for you, Nathanial. Try not to give him a hard time."

Nathanial bit his lip. "Ok," he said hesitantly. He didn't want to give Boss a hard time, but Boss just didn't make it easy—he was too secretive to trust. "I'm supposed to have a lesson with him in a few minutes."

"Well, then you better go. You don't want to be late! Thanks for calling sweetheart. I love you."

"I love you, too, mom. I'm not sure when I can call again, but I'll try soon."

"Oh, I know you only get phone privileges once a week. It's ok. Don't you worry about me, baby. Just have a good time."

"Thanks, mom. You're the best."

"So are you, sweetie. Talk to you later. Bye-bye."

"Bye."

Nathanial heard the phone click off and he sat back heavily. He knew she was being strong for him. He missed her. She was the only friend he had before his twelfth birthday, when he had met Aliya.

He pulled his hand back from the desk tablet and the screen changed back to the portal home page. He skimmed the symbols for each of his classes lining the left side. He touched the circular *GE* and the notes for General Education popped up. He hit the back arrow and touched the *FS* symbol, curious as to what notes Factory Safety could have.

He saw the explanation of uses for the earwax he'd collected and took out his notebook to jot some down.

Pulling the glass pen from the notebook spine, he wondered how the ink could come out of its twisted tip. He put the point on the page and jokingly thought *dear diary*. Astonishingly, the little specks on the page gathered like bits of metal on a magnet and the word dear diary appeared beneath the pen.

Nathanial quickly pulled his writing hand up and said, "Whoa." He looked from the portal's notes and back to the notebook. "Ok, let's try this again."

Placing the pen under the words *dear diary*, Nathanial read the uses of earwax from the portal. As he did so, the specks gathered on the notebook page to write the words:

Earwax is most commonly used as a leak stopper in a variety of sprite household objects. Whether it be a bucket, a sitting pool, or a spitting straw, earwax can plug up that annoying leak. A lesser-known use for earwax, though almost every sprite unknowingly uses it, is within the ingredients for hair gel. It's the perfect shiny semi-solid to keep frisky hair in place.

Nathanial laughed and the words *sprites are weird* showed up at the bottom of the page.

Deciding he'd better get down the tree, he changed his clothes into his casual wear. He put the notebook into one pants pocket and the battle blade in the other. On the way out, Nathanial slipped on the hoodie Boss had given him the day before and closed the door behind him.

Chapter Thirteen

ANOTHER ROUND WITH BOSS

*N*athanial didn't have any problems with the glider this time. The student helper who strapped him in was a different sprite who obviously didn't take the same joy in taunting newbies as the other had, which allowed Nathanial to keep his aggression focused on Boss. He used the left and right handles above him like a pro around the curves of the tree. It might have been helpful that he was acting on instinct. His thoughts about what he was going to say to Boss were keeping him from paying attention to the descent, and he found himself surprised when the glider had reached its stop at the bottom of Hyperion.

The student helper at the base assisted him out of the harness and he walked coolly up to Boss.

"Nicely done," Boss said with a smile.

Nathanial was surprised to see Boss had a sword attached to his hip, which distracted his attention and unfairly threw out all of the dialogue he'd planned for this moment.

"Let's go," Boss said, and they moved along the

same trail as the day before.

Nathanial followed in silence. He wanted to ask about the blood and why Boss hadn't warned him that sprites bled differently. He'd planned to be confrontational in order to get it through Boss's thick skull, that hiding information like that from him could have led the century kids to discover he was human. Since Boss now had a sword, he tried to think of a nicer way to put it.

They reached a clearing and Boss unsheathed his sword. "I brought my old friend here to start your sword training, even if you can't command your battle blade into this state yet, it'll be good to get you started on how to use it." Boss held out his hand. "Hand me the blade and I'll shape it for you."

Nathanial took the sheathed blade from his pocket and pulled it out as a sword like Mary Poppins with a lamp from her bag.

Boss was speechless, which Nathanial had thought to be impossible. He quite enjoyed the effect.

"You must have had some lengthy conversations with that blade last night," Boss finally said with a chuckle.

"I guess so." Nathanial spoke deliberately. "And

now it's time for sword training? To deter hungry tongues?"

Boss nodded, obviously contemplating the narrowed eyes of Nathanial.

"Are you sure that's a good idea? Aren't you afraid I'll *cut myself*?" Nathanial asked, emphasizing the last two words like a chess player yelling *checkmate*!

"We'll be careful," Boss said, clearly not picking up on the implication so Nathanial tried again.

"But if I did, someone might see my *red* blood."

Boss dropped his shoulders with realization. "Nathanial, don't be so dramatic."

"Dramatic? I'm not being dramatic. It would just have been nice to know sprites bleed white so that I'd know to hide my scratches from the century kids who just happen to hate humans, but seem to want to hang around one all day."

"Not all sprites bleed white."

"What?"

"That's why I didn't tell you. It's not that big of a deal."

Nathanial didn't believe it.

"True, usually blood change comes with the skin pigment change," Boss said bobbling his head side to side.

"Aha! I knew it. So you were hiding it. It would have been a dead giveaway if they saw my blood was red, wouldn't it?"

"No. You're not so pale. You could be interpreted as coloring early."

"Ugh." Nathanial shook his head, frustrated.

"So, do you want to train or keep whining?"

Nathanial was fuming. He almost brought up Boss's hiding Aliya from him, just to try compounding the proof of lies, but he bit his tongue. If Boss knew he knew about Aliya, then he'd know Nathanial was planning to go after her. So instead of pushing it, he just lifted his sword.

"Fine," Nathanial huffed. "I could use the outlet right now." He pointed the sharp blade at Boss.

Boss merely sighed into a chuckle and lifted his sword.

For the next hour, Nathanial learned the basics of how to hold a sword. He couldn't imagine there would be so much technique in just holding a sword and thought Boss was just being too picky about it. But once he started swinging it to form perfect arcs, he found out why it needed to be held in perfect balance. If he held it wrong, then his elbow would twist and he wouldn't be able to swing in consecutive arcs without dropping it.

When the sun began to fall, Boss called it quits.

"Not bad for your first time," Boss said as they walked the trail returning to the air-shoots.

Nathanial sighed, too tired to harp on his trust issues with Boss, and just said, "Thanks."

"Did you call your mom?"

"Yeah."

"How's she doing?"

Nathanial looked up at him suspiciously. "Fine. Why?"

"Just making conversation."

Nathanial sighed again then said, "She misses me."

"Of course she does. She's your mom."

Nathanial remembered Mila saying Boss was like his guardian here and wondered if he really would be willing to give him some money. Boss saw Nathanial's contemplations and asked, "What?"

"Eh," Nathanial hovered not feeling right about asking after being so hot tempered before, "my friend wants me to go to the market with her."

"Oh, yeah?"

Nathanial nodded slowly. "Yeah, but, ah…"

"But you don't have any coin."

"Right." Nathanial winced.

Boss reached into his pocket and pulled out a

coin sack. He loosened the strings and poured out pieces of silver and gold.

"The values are pretty self-explanatory," Boss said ordering the pieces from biggest to smallest. "Gold is rare, making it the most valuable, much like it is in your own civilization, so the bigger the better. There are three sizes of gold and four sizes of silver. Most trinkets will only cost a few silver. The price tags will have color-coated pictures to represent the costs, so you shouldn't have a problem." He dumped the coins back in the sack and handed it to Nathanial.

"Wow," Nathanial said looking at it with surprise. "Thanks." He felt a pang of guilt that he planned to use the money on a running-away outfit. It made him wonder who was really the less trustworthy of the two of them. But then he remembered if Boss had just been up-front with him about Aliya in the first place, then maybe he wouldn't be feeling the need to hide his rescue plan from him, so, he decided, it was Boss's own fault really.

"So, who is this friend of yours?" Boss asked with a smirk.

"Just a girl from class." Nathanial saw Boss's growing smile. Nathanial rolled his eyes. "It's not like that. Spassel is coming, too. It's not a date or anything."

Boss nodded. "Ok, have fun. Try the skitzel while you're there. It's kind of like a pretzel with a punch."

MARKET DAY

*T*he next few days went smooth enough as Nathanial fell into a routine of classes. He had figured out how to set his alarm through the Hyperion Portal and woke daily to a soft vibration in his bed that made him feel fresh in the morning.

Although he had tried to give Mila back the tap-aid necklace the day after the leaning-tree incident, she'd refused to take it. She said he needed it to keep up with the sprites and to just loosen up on any vibration that heats the amulet. This meant he was quickly becoming teacher's pet in many of his classes, and it seemed to confirm for Bron that there was no way Nathanial could ever have been human.

The ever-mounting anxiety to get on the road to find Aliya was a daily struggle, however. Mila had pleaded with Nathanial to stop asking if she'd heard anything about his travel papers. He'd attempted to formulate a new plan to get them on the move, but Mila stifled it by saying, "Do you want me to be your guide or not? Now stuff it and trust me that I know what I'm doing."

When trying to avoid thinking about Aliya, he shifted his energy to solving the surprising mystery that Spassel had become. He still refused to tell Nathanial what his dream job was, and he seemed embarrassed about the club he was part of. He disappeared after every third period to meet with his club and would not tell Nathanial anything more about it.

When the weekend rolled around, Nathanial found Mila and himself waiting at the skitzel stand for Spassel who was a record five minutes late.

"What happened to 'on time is late'?" Nathanial mumbled looking at the time glowing from a Hyperion Portal access point set between two shops in the tree.

"Sorry, guys..." Spassel was panting as he pulled out of a full-on run. "Lost track of time. We were having quite the role play. Almost forgot myself."

Nathanial snorted, still picturing Spassel's club as some sort of Dungeons and Dragons gaming group. Spassel's claim of having no creativity was way off if something of that sort *was* taking place.

"Oh, are we having skitzel?" Spassel continued, catching his breath and pulling out his coin, "Let me get this for my apologies. I'm starving."

Nathanial took the twisted food that was

knotted up in three different layers of powder-coated bread: it was green at the top, then orange, and yellow at its base. He sniffed the food sending his nose into a tingle fit.

Mila appeared to be containing her amusement, as her amethyst-colored eyes gave a twinkle his way.

Nathanial, of course, didn't trust it and lowered the skitzel at once. "What?"

"Nothing," Mila said, quickly turning her attention to her own and taking a large confident bite.

Spassel was already to the second orangey knot by this point. "Haven't you ever had a skitzel?"

Nathanial shrugged. "No." He took a bite.

The journey his mouth was about to undertake began slowly. With a few short chews on the soft dissolving bread, it didn't seem like he had swallowed very much. Then it happened. From paprika, to jalapeños, to the fires of brimstone, his jaw dropped and his eyes watered. He began to search frantically at all the different concession stands for a cure.

"What are you doing?" Spassel followed Nathanial from stand to stand, licking his fingers, having eaten the entirety of his own skitzel.

"Water, I need water," Nathanial said passing

food stand after food stand.

Mila sniggered and chomped her way through half her skitzel.

"You don't need water," Spassel said trying to stop Nathanial. "You just need to finish the skitzel."

"Are you crazy?!" Nathanial exclaimed, keeping his mouth open.

"Trust me," Spassel said. "It's the way the skitzel is designed."

Nathanial looked from Spassel's honest face to Mila, contently licking her fingers.

Taking another bite seemed like suicide. He didn't know if he could force himself to do it, even if he believed Spassel. The pain had reached his stomach and was surely morphing into a pot of knives.

"I can't," Nathanial said shaking his head. "I need to find some water."

"Nat…" Spassel gripped onto Nathanial's shoulders, "It's a test of will. You have to finish the skitzel. It's its own remedy. Nothing else. It will only get worse if you don't finish it."

Feeling now like his head was about to explode, and his stomach was twisting around a blade, Nathanial closed his eyes and took another bite. There was no relief.

"It's…not…working…" Nathanial moaned.

The crowd had begun to stop and stare at Nathanial. They seemed uncertain whether to be confused, amused, or concerned.

"Keep going, Nat," Mila said seriously.

Nathanial quickly took another bite, then another, then another. Before he knew it, the skitzel was gone and the pain with it. He wiped his eyes clear and filled his lungs with a relieving breath. "Oh, my god," he said coming out of his shock, "I feel like I gave birth to a fire baby out of my mouth."

Spassel snorted and shook his head. "I can't believe you've never had a skitzel." He walked toward an adjacent shop. "That's like a toddler training food."

The crowd looked amusedly reassured and went back to their shopping. Mila patted Nathanial on the back. "Let's go get you some baby clothes, I mean some civvy clothes," she shook her head in mock mistake.

Nathanial growled as he followed her into a shop. Boss was really going to get an earful for this one.

The sprite-clothing store was not exactly what Nathanial had been expecting. He'd been in one before, in Midtown with Aliya the year before. They had been looking for a good sprite disguise.

That store had had rows of hanging shirts, pants, and jackets like any good clothing store should. This place was stacked with materials. Spools of yarn, bins of buttons, racks of embellishments piled up with twigs, safety pins, colorful pebbles, and fuzzy bobbles all filled the shop.

"Ugh," Nathanial said halting a few steps in. "Are we expected to make our own clothes here?"

Mila put her arm around his shoulder and admired the store from beside him. "No, but you do make your own identity here. Pick out the kind of things that catch your eye, and give them to one of the designers in the back." She pushed a basket into Nathanial's hands. "They'll size you up and spin you something in two shakes of a lamb's tail." She swung up her own basket and swished her way into the colorful aisles.

Nathanial gulped. "Oh, Bunny, where are you when I need you?" he asked aloud, recalling how she'd been the best at dressing him up before adventures, but when she didn't pop out from behind one of the shelves, he began to peruse the store. "Okay, just grab some things that catch your eye. Making my own identity. Here we go."

That's when Nathanial spotted a shelf against the wall marked with an overhead sign that read,

Don't waste time, pick your style on a dime, just take one from each line!

That sounded promising. Nathanial rushed over and licked his lips. "Okay, let's see," he said, examining the store's layout a little closer.

From looking at the picture representations on each row, it seemed the idea was to choose a shirt fabric from one vertical row of patterned swatches, and from another vertical row a choice for the kind of bottoms, represented by a picture of pants, shorts, skirts, and even overalls. The row next to that were pocket choices and next to those were zippers and buttons.

Nathanial picked up a shirt swatch. It was shimmery blue with dark velvety crisscrosses. A tag on it pictured three silver circles engraved with *M*s. Nathanial pulled out the money sack and scooped out a few silver pieces. Letters were indeed engraved into the coins and *M* was marked on the third from the largest coin that he had. There seemed to be plenty of those in the sack, so he threw the swatch into his basket. This gave him a surprising feeling of exhilaration. He moved onto the row for bottoms and proceeded to riffle through the fabrics there.

Once he'd picked something from each row, he glanced around the shop in search of the designers Mila had described. He spotted a sign near the back that read, MAKE IT SEW, and went to see what trial awaited him next.

Four lady sprites and one male sprite stood in flamboyant attire behind a long desk that was covered with fabrics. Mila was already being measured by a sprite who wore a dress composed of sprite sized Skittles when the boa-wearing, top-hatted, bedazzle-suited prince of a sprite spotted Nathanial with his basket and yelled, "Dibs!" while pointing a black-polished nail at him.

Like a whirlwind, the princely sprite spun around Nathanial with a measuring tape and scissors. He pinned together fabrics from spools that matched the swatches out of the basket and he held up pockets, eyeing for their best placement.

Suddenly there was a Nathanial-sized mannequin spinning in front of him and the clothes came together in time-lapse like speed on it. The princely tailor was a blur of stars.

"Voilà!" the master of needle and thread exclaimed with his arms out in presentation for Nathanial to approve the masterpiece.

"Wow," Nathanial said, honestly impressed.

The outfit may have looked like something out of a disco party with its light-catching blue button-up collared shirt and multi-pocketed loose-fit brown pants, but it wasn't far off from what Nathanial remembered Bunny picking out for him in Midtown, so he was happy with it.

"What do you think?" he asked Mila who had just joined him and leaned her elbow up on his shoulder.

She wore a crooked smile and said, "Oh, yeah, definitely you." Then she patted him on the back and said, "I'm going to go check on Spaz. He's been in that changing room way too long."

"I'll bag everything up for you then, shall I?" The tailor asked with an accomplished smile and small bow.

"Yes, please," Nathanial answered gratefully and then went over to join Mila by the changing rooms.

Spassel's little shifting feet could just be seen underneath the frilly curtain.

"Oh, Spaassell…what's taking you so long in there, buddy?" Mila asked and leaned back against the center of the three-way mirror.

"I can't decide on what to wear."

"On what to wear…to what?" Mila checked to see if Nathanial had a clue. He just shrugged.

Spassel was quiet for a while until he said, "To Factory Safety class."

The light bulb lit up in Nathanial's head and he burst out laughing. Mila stood up straight and looked at him quizzically. Nathanial held up a finger and said, "Flori *was* mentioning how she preferred feathers for making humans sneeze rather than catching a vibration in the nasal cavity. Why don't you get one of those boas like my tailor is wearing?"

Mila gasped in delight. Spassel pushed aside the curtain and walked out in a pout. Mila pulled Spassel into a headlock and said, "Spaz, you old cricket you! Are you playing songs on two fiddles?"

"What?" Spassel pulled out of her grasp and combed his fingers through his hair. "No, what are you talking about?"

"I thought you were with," Mila snapped her fingers in thought, "what's her name, from your club, Kadee?"

"Kadee!" Spassel exclaimed in shock. "No way! We're just friends!"

Nathanial and Mila shared in a good giggle fit.

"It's pointless anyway," Spassel said while hanging up the tasseled cowboy-like shirt he had tried on. "The most I could do is decorate my school uniform and I quite like the way it is naturally."

He tugged at the collar of his school blazer.

Mila lifted her brow and said, "Yeah, well, Spaz, you might look good in your uniform, but you should really mix things up on the weekend." She picked the cowboy shirt back up off the hanger and added, "I'm getting this for you." She folded the shirt over her arm that was already draped with several dark purple garments that shone with leather-like textures and silver buttons.

They purchased their merchandise in good humor and headed out to explore the rest of the marketplace.

An hour or more zipped by before Nathanial was back in his room with his haul. Mila stood in the doorframe, waving goodbye to Spassel who also had bags dangling from his elbows.

"Mind if I come in for a minute," she asked, having watched Spassel enter his room a few doors down and checking that the hallway was clear.

"Sure," Nathanial said, preoccupied with pulling out his freshly tailored clothing and his new rucksack.

The door closed and Mila stood quietly. Nathanial stopped and turned toward her. She looked concerned.

"What's up?" Nathanial asked with a crinkled brow.

Mila inhaled slowly. She seemed unsure where to start, and then she said, "Well, you know how I keep saying we're sticking with the plan, you know, to get travel papers for Niche hopping?"

Nathanial narrowed his eyes. "Yeah…?"

"Yeah, we still are but…I've had to form a backup plan."

Nathanial pursed his lips. She'd been telling him to shut-it all week about a backup plan. "What's changed?"

"It doesn't usually take this long to get papers forged, but that's not what's bothering me. There could be a dozen reasons why the papers are late."

"Then what is it?" Nathanial urged.

"It's Kale."

"You said not to worry about him—that his kind has always had it out for yours," Nathanial said.

"I know, but I've been watching his hate toward you intensify all week. Usually, he can block me from seeing his thoughts and emotions, but his despising you is radiating beyond that. With how well you are doing in class, Bron has basically replaced him with you as his number one. There's bound to be some jealousy issues there."

Nathanial groaned then said with attempted optimism, "Yeah, but, I mean, what's he going to do? He can't do anything as long as Bron has my back."

"Which is exactly why he's been following you so closely the last couple of days. He's looking for proof that you are the human changeling. Look, my point is, I want you to keep that rucksack on you, loaded with all the things I helped you pick out today and any gear you think you might need on the road. Pack your travel clothes and that water canister. It can pull water out of any living plant. It was a great find!"

She sighed and continued. "We aren't attached at the hip, so if you find yourself needing to make a run for it when I'm not around, just head up toward the transport station and I'll meet you there."

"How will you know...?"

"I'll know," she cut in.

"Why don't we just go now? Why wait for Kale to find me out?"

"Because it's too dangerous. This is an emergency-only plan, ok? The papers should be ready any day now."

Nathanial opened his mouth, but Mila held up her hand. She turned to the door, put her ear on it as if listening, and then quickly slipped out of the room.

Nathanial remained with his mouth opened,

then deflated into his chair. He swiveled toward his desk and began to arrange his ready-to-flee items.

"Travel clothes..." He put the still-folded disco attire into the new rucksack. "Gear..." He flung his geckite gloves in. "Water canister..." He pulled it out from a cloth shopping bag and added it to the pile. "I should grab some food at some point, too. What else?"

Nathanial began opening drawers to see what he might want to take on the run. He found and added Bunny's dust bag, his ear cuffs, a few socks, and underwear. He contemplated the pine body spray Spassel had used on him his first day, in case there were no showers on the trip, and chucked it in. Then he lifted his old balled-up human clothes out from the drawer and added them to the rucksack just in case he found a chance to go see his mom.

Out of his pants pockets he pulled the notebook and his battle blade. He set the knife down and procrastinated by flipping through the notebook. The inside cover page had self-populated with: These thoughts belong to Nathanial Thatcher; a strange symbol that reminded him of the Egyptian eye of Ra was printed under the words with a few extra circular embellishments around it.

During the week, he had filled about a dozen

pages with the more interesting facts from classes, and especially made sure to jot down any tap commands that could assist in manipulating the world around him. He smiled and read what Mr. P had called an old proverb for finding grubs in a tree:

> When in a pinch for a bite,
> and no market be in sight
> Just put an ear to the bark,
> or call upon a friendly lark
> For either way you shall find,
> your tummy full of squirmy kind

Nathanial shook his head reading what the pen had self-populated as an afterthought:

> Shoot me down if ever I'm,
> in need of this stupid rhyme.

He flipped quickly past more school notes until he came to the pages that reflected the fear he harbored after losing his memories. He never wanted to forget again, but in case he did, he wanted this to be his backup. Many pages recounted the three-day journey with Boss, Phlegm, and Bunny, where he battled to retain his health and help Aliya. He stopped on the page where he had let the pen try to sketch Aliya's face from his memory. It wasn't half bad, but he wished he had seen her smile more. The eyes were so sorrowful. Strangely, the pen had also jotted phrases of Aliya's sporadically around the page. He had no idea he had been thinking them as they formed.

> You can't trust the sprites. They use humans for their own gain. We have to stick together.

At the bottom of the page, Nathanial scratched at the words:

> What will she think of me when she sees I'm a sprite?

"I have to ask Boss how to erase things out of this crazy book," he said getting to his feet and putting both the notebook and battle blade back into their respective pants pockets.

Glancing at the time on the portal, Nathanial slung the rucksack over his shoulder and headed down to see Boss. Just because it was the weekend didn't mean he could skip his lessons with Boss, or so he'd been told.

"How was the market?" Boss asked as they walked the trail to the training area.

Nathanial was ready to rant about the skitzel, but Boss wasn't finished.

"See you got a new rucksack. It's nice," Boss pulled on the sturdy multi-material bag slung over Nathanial's shoulder. "I'm surprised I didn't see you at the marketplace. You couldn't have spent much time hanging around. I was there for a few hours this morning."

"We only went a couple hours ago," Nathanial managed to squeeze in and took another breath to talk about the skitzel.

"I see, late risers. Understandable on a weekend," Boss said. "I got you something."

They entered the clearing and Boss walked over to a mahogany wooden box atop a protruding tree root.

"You did?" Nathanial pouted as he joined Boss and took the box that was offered. It wouldn't be very polite to yell at someone who was giving you a present.

Nathanial lifted the hooked latch, and opened the box. Inside were two beautifully detailed leather straps with silver buckles.

"Is this," Nathanial said, picking up one of the straps in awe, "is this for the battle blade?"

"Yes," Boss said picking up the second strap proudly. "The sheath has loops for them. You can strap the battle blade to your ankle. Hyperion clothes are notorious for developing holes in their pockets, you don't want to keep something so valuable in them."

The words rushed over Nathanial like an omen. He sat the box and strap down onto the tree root and felt both his pockets. He pulled the battle blade from one with relief but from the other...

"My notebook," he said feeling a twist in his gut. All those ridiculous, absentminded, *human* thoughts that were scribbled in with his notes, *and* his name was on it! "I have to find it!"

"Wait!" Boss said grabbing Nathanial's turning shoulder. "You've got what, a week's worth of notes in there? You probably lost it on the glide down. There's no finding that. You can get another notebook. Come on, we need to train."

"No, you don't understand," but as Nathanial looked into Boss's growing concern he bit his tongue. How much would he have to divulge if he expressed the fear he had of someone finding the notebook?

"What don't I understand?" Boss stiffened.

Nathanial gulped. "Nothing..." he finally stammered. He couldn't risk Boss helping him find the notebook and then seeing he had his memories back. He'd surely put him on lockdown to keep him from Aliya. "You're right. I can get another one."

Boss nodded and pulled out his sword.

Though Nathanial was distracted during the next fifteen minutes, his amulet always seemed to have a way of picking up the slack. He'd had a week's worth of sword training now, and it'd only seem to take a couple of adjustments from any advice Boss gave for him in order to pick up on how best to defend or attack.

Now Boss was getting out of breath as neither he nor Nathanial had made a mistake in quite a few sword-swinging moves. This frustration gave way to Boss using a maneuver that he hadn't yet shown nor taught Nathanial. Boss lunged, twisted, and swiveled his weapon along Nathanial's, sending his battle blade up into the air in an arc. It landed some fifteen feet away in the moss.

"Hey!" Nathanial protested. "Not fair!"

Boss seemed both satisfied and concerned as he aimed to catch his breath. He walked awkwardly over to the bench that was carved into a root, stretching and cracking his back. Then he sat down and drank from one of the water bottles there. "Have a seat," he motioned next to him. "We need to talk."

Those words never seemed to bode well, so it

was with a heavy posture that Nathanial complied. Boss handed him the second water bottle and Nathanial drank slowly, waiting for the lecture.

"Don't think I haven't noticed how quickly you're picking this up," Boss said. He waited for Nathanial to respond, but the water bottle didn't leave his lips. "At first I thought it must have something to do with the way Bunny tapped the blade for you. Maybe she'd put a little bit too much of her own ambition into the blade's vein and that was giving you the extra kick."

Nathanial lowered the bottle with interested contemplation.

"You remember what I told you about how the battle blade works?" Boss responded to the look. Nathanial screwed up his face trying to remember. Boss sniggered and continued. "I told you that the battle blade was designed for a human to use through the will of a sprite. This is because without the sprite tapping the blade, a human could do nothing more with it than use it as a knife. But besides that, there also has to be a natural quality within the human, like bravery, for instance, in order for the tap to transfer abilities from the sprite to the human. It cannot be wielded without this sprite/human combination…usually."

"Usually?" Nathanial mimicked.

"You were a human when you received the blade and Bunny needed to activate it for you. But now..."

"Now I'm a sprite."

"Yes. So, is the blade still acting on Bunny's tap or has your own mixed vibration taken over? If her influence is still a part of the equation, then there could be a double-sprite, part-human chemistry taking place within it. That could explain how you've been picking up these sword techniques so quickly, or that's what I had thought until..."

"Until?" Nathanial pressed.

"...until I spoke with your teachers."

Nathanial felt his heart quicken and the amulet gain weight around his neck.

"It seems your quick study is not limited to the battle blade." Boss waited. Nathanial did not respond. "Phlegm said that on instruction to feel for a vibration, it looked like you were actually tapping into the vibration, before you ever even had a class on tapping."

Nathanial thought back on that day with confusion. He didn't have the amulet with the flying squirrel, right?

Boss continued, "And Mr. Bones says it's like you can see the vibrations tapped without having to open your eyes to the ones glowing in front of you."

Worry scurried about in Nathanial at the apparent proclamation that his way of catching, tapping, and tricking vibrations was not normal. He supposed he should have realized it. After all, the entire point of tapping a vibration was to see it physically, but he could see it behind his eyes already. He knew that the amulet had only magnified this strange element that was already in him, because he had begun to see something spark on that very first encounter with vibrations in the Niche with Boss and then, yes, definitely with the squirrel in Mr. P's class.

Unfortunately, he knew Boss's point was how Nathanial was turning out to be such a quick study and he feared the consequences of revealing the amulet that he credited this to.

He waited for Boss to *continue* until it was clear he was waiting for Nathanial's response.

"Well," Nathanial thought very carefully about how to proceed. "I think you must be right."

Boss lifted a brow.

Nathanial continued. "It must be because I'm a changeling. And my vibrations are all juiced up, because of Bunny. Maybe the battle blade is helping me in my classes, too. Is that possible?" Nathanial crossed his fingers mentally.

Boss's expression seemed to have petrified momentarily. Nathanial feared Boss might already know the truth about the amulet. Maybe he was just trying to get Nathanial to confess.

Then without so much as a flinch Boss said, "Maybe."

Nathanial relaxed. Boss stood and capped his water bottle.

"Hey, now, I have something I've been wanting to talk to you about, too." Nathanial said in truth and in need of a diversion. "Why did you want me to try that skitzel? It was horrible!"

"Oh, good, I'm glad you tried it!" Boss laughed. "You needed to try it! It's one of the staples of growing up sprite. It's crucial to learn mind-over-body disciplines. Your body will refuse a second bite, as it wants nothing more than to refuse the pain—but your mind must order you to finish the food to resolve the problem."

"Mm-hmm." Nathanial rolled his eyes then lit up with another question. "Also, how do you know how to fight so amazingly?"

Boss smiled down at Nathanial. "Thanks for the compliment, but I can't explain."

"Why not?" Nathanial asked downhearted.

"I think you keep forgetting that I'm cursed." Boss said wiping his sweaty palms on his jacket.

"Wait— That's for real?"

"Afraid so." Boss nodded.

"What does that mean exactly?"

"It means there are a lot of things about myself that I can never share with another living soul for as long as I live."

Nathanial frowned. Was he being serious?

Boss retrieved the battle blade from the moss and returned it to Nathanial. "That's enough for this weekend," Boss said with an emotional fatigue that seemed to outweigh the physical. "We'll hit it hard again on Monday."

After narrowly escaping the discovery of the illegal crutch around his neck, Nathanial rushed up various air-shoots along the glider path in hopes to avoid the discovery of his other secret. He hopelessly searched hundreds of mossy branches for any sign of the notebook. If he had dropped it from the glider, it was unlikely anyone was going to find it, but he wanted to be sure.

Exhausted and starving he stumbled into the cafeteria at nightfall. He was still so distracted that he ate all of his stew before curiosity over its hairy texture motivated him enough to read the label on the cart he'd taken it from: *Owl Pellet Gruel.* Nathanial thought he might be sick and retired for the night.

Chapter Fifteen

CREDENCE JUNCTION

*T*he next morning, while skimming his third hallway with *retrace your steps* in mind, Nathanial saw Spassel turning a corner. Was that a suit of armor he was wearing? On feathered feet, Nathanial ran down the hall to peek around the corner. It led outside onto a branch where just the tip of Spassel's cape could be seen vanishing into the high green brush. Nathanial's excitement spiked. Was he finally going to see what this mysterious club was all about?

Keeping on his tiptoes, he dashed along the trail. He could hear shouts and hollow impacts getting louder. Nathanial approached a clearing and darted into the towering foliage so as not to be seen by the dozen colliding figures. He knelt down behind a tree knot with just the right size peephole to spy from.

Three sets of boys were in the middle of full-blown cosplay with wooden swords and battle armor made of leather and…nutshells?

"I knew it, Dungeons and Dragons…" Nathanial

snickered to himself.

He then noticed there was actually a girl playing, too. Could that be the Kadee that Mila had teased Spassel about? She was sitting on a mushroom wearing a pretty dress verging on a ball gown, her hair was twisted up in a beehive, and she had fashioned a crown out of flower petals. She was looking down at the boys like they were fighting for her—and as if they rightfully should be.

Nathanial was just beginning to wonder where Spassel was when he entered the scene with his wooden sword aloft from behind the mushroom on a little hill.

"Enough," Spassel demanded, and the boys stopped fighting. "Too much sprite blood has been spilled over this folly of a cause. What will it take to make you all see there is no reason for hate between us? If our blood traits rank us high or low, do we not still share a common bloodline? Look back far enough and every living thing shares the root that sprung out into all of us. You fight as if you are fighting something that is other, like that *other* is not part of yourself. All of you are capable of seeing what the other side is willing to sacrifice so that their children may have a chance at a worthy future. So for that future I ask you now, is it not time we put down our swords and find a compromise, or are you willing to pass your weapons on to your children when you fall?"

All the boys laid down their swords. The girl slipped off her mushroom and approached Spassel.

"Wow, go Spassel. End the war and get the girl!" Nathanial said impressed just before he felt a sharp poke in the back.

"Not exactly," a sprite in cosplay said, with a wooden sword at Nathanial's back.

Nathanial slowly got to his feet with his hands up.

"Move it," the sprite said with a thrust of the sword.

"Ouch!" Nathanial groaned and moved into the opening. "Calm down, Sir Pokes-a-lot." But Nathanial looked again and saw it was actually a girl sprite with her hair pulled up into her nut helmet. He corrected himself, "Lady Pokes-a-lot."

It looked as though an ambush had been planned, as more sprites came into the clearing from all directions. Their eyes fell onto Nathanial.

"Hey," one of the sprites in the middle griped, "I don't remember there being a spy caught in all this."

Spassel jumped down from the hill and walked toward the prisoner. "No, there wasn't. That's just my friend Nat."

"Spassel! No outsiders allowed!" Protested another sprite. "It ruins the authenticity."

"I know," Spassel said disparagingly taking ahold of Nathanial's arm to escort him out. "I was about to die anyway. Go on without me."

The sounds of fighting quickly resumed as Spassel let go of Nathanial's arm along the return trail.

"I don't know why you say you aren't creative," Nathanial finally said, "pretending to be knights fighting over a princess is about as creative as you can get."

"What?" Spassel crinkled his nose. "We were role-playing. There's no need for creativity. We just pick the part of a historical figure and do what they did. We are actually called debate club because during the week we deliberate between the opposing sides of the previous weekend's fights—talk about which side was right or wrong.

"Right," Nathanial nodded while still processing Spassel's hasty explanation. "Either way, it's nothing to be embarrassed about."

Spassel sighed and looked over to Nathanial with a contemplative expression. "You're not like most sprites," he finally said.

Nathanial gulped. "Why do you say that?"

"You don't have the natural reservations most

of us do. You should know why I'm embarrassed. First because I told you my parents are yellow and now because you caught me playing one of the bravest heroes of all time when clearly that role should be portrayed by an orange sprite. You've probably even figured out what I see my inner calling as and have no protest against that either."

"Mm…" Nathanial pursed his lips and nodded. Spassel examined Nathanial's face.

"Head council member," Spassel finally admitted. Nathanial raised an eyebrow and Spassel continued. "I think it's my best shot at making a real difference. The current head of the council has done a pretty good job. Hyperion wouldn't be here without him, but I think he's afraid of making the big calls for change. For instance, these rumors going around that the council allowed a human who changed into a sprite to attend school at Hyperion…"

Nathanial's heart skipped a beat. Was he about to find out that his funny little friend was biased against him?

"It shouldn't just be a rumor. That leads to further distrust of the head councilor. He should stand up and admit proudly if he has indeed made that decision, but he is too afraid of causing unrest. He probably also fears it would put the changeling in danger, but if everyone knew the identity of the changeling, he would be too famous to touch. Sure, there would be protests. High-profile groups, like the Swartza, would lead them, but at least then they would have to be open about it. They couldn't just take the changeling to do whatever they like with. Too many sprites are switching to factory-friendly products— that don't harm the factories— to be okay with letting the one who changed into a sprite go missing without taking notice. But as it stands now, no one is openly saying anything because no one really knows what's going on in our government anymore."

Nathanial nodded his head in relief. Spassel was smart and in a deeper way than books alone can teach.

"It's going to take some new blood in that council if we want to get rid of the old way of running things," Spassel finally concluded and defiantly crossed his arms.

Nathanial smiled. It sounded like Spassel was going to run for sprite president one day, and he could definitely get down with his platform.

"That's great, Spassel," Nathanial said patting him on the back. "I'll vote for you."

Spassel beamed like midday sunshine bursting through a rained-out storm cloud.

They were rounding the dormitory hall when both of them stopped. Bron, Kale, Jax, Sil, and four other older boys with budding colors all stood in front of Nathanial's door. Nathanial's heart kerplunked into his stomach. Bron was holding Nathanial's notebook; Kale was grinning like a mad hyena.

Nathanial put a hand on Spassel's chest and slowly started to push him back around the corner. Just before he was safely out of view, he saw Mila. She was huffing on the other side of the century kids. They all turned toward her. She made eye contact with Nathanial and then snatched the notebook out of Bron's hand and took off in the opposite direction. The century kids went after her. Nathanial instinctively moved to help her, but Spassel grabbed hold of his rucksack.

"What are you doing?" Spassel shouted.

Nathanial took that second to think. The backup plan was in effect. Mila would head up to the transport station. Then, with a shock, he noticed that Kale had stayed behind and he had apparently heard Spassel because he was looking right at him.

"Spassel, get out of here!" Nathanial bellowed as he pushed Spassel away and dove for the adjacent air-shoot.

Nathanial came out of the shoot on a middle

balcony of the central pagoda. He looked up at the dizzying heights and ran up the nearest set of stairs. Up, he just needed to keep going up. He took a chance to glance back and saw Kale exit the air-shoot and sprout his wings.

"Right," Nathanial panicked and scanned around for another shoot. He found one and dove in.

On his next exit, he slammed into Mila and sent them both tumbling onto the ground. They scurried back to their feet and continued around the curved balcony. Nathanial saw that Bron and Sil flew between the balconies, just yards above Kale, all eyes on him and moments from catching up. Mila pushed Nathanial into another air-shoot and he shockingly watched her dive toward a far balcony before the tube blocked his vision.

This shoot put Nathanial out on the top tier of the pagoda. He looked down at all the century kids either popping out of various shoots or flying up the center. Mila was nowhere in sight. Next to him an arrowed sign reading *Hyperion Transport Station* pointed out onto a branch. He ran for it.

Nathanial's heart took a chance, feeling relief and excitement, when he saw the marked doors that would lead him to his salvation. He was almost in the transport hub when he heard a loud whistle to his right. He looked to see Mila pulling two fingers from her lips. She was out on something like a helipad, but instead of a painted H, there was an imprint of a bird. Mila stood by a bright-orange–feathered friend with black-and-white wings. She hopped onto the bird's neck and waved for Nathanial to join her. He dashed over and jumped on behind her.

"Nat this is Ori. Ori, meet Nat," Mila introduced them while handing Nathanial's notebook back to him. The bird twisted its head around to tweet at him.

Nathanial gulped, caught his breath, and stuffed the notebook into his rucksack while managing to say, "Hey…Ori."

Mila kicked her heels and the bird flapped into the air. Nathanial looked down as they rose and saw Bron and Kale shaking their fists as the rest of the century kids clumped up around them.

"Why aren't they flying after us?" Nathanial asked.

"Would you chase after these chompers?" She pointed to the bird's beak.

Nathanial knew she had a point.

"Ok, girl," Mila said patting the bird's head, "Credence Junction."

With a lurch, they picked up speed. Nathanial

had to hold tight around Mila's waist and squeeze his aching legs against the bird's neck, but after a few minutes of unstable flapping, Ori leveled out and Nathanial loosened up.

Even though Nathanial knew he should be feeling scared or worried or disappointed at his secret being out at Hyperion, he couldn't help but smile. He was finally on his way toward Aliya.

They flew south, keeping the ocean on their right until the sun was almost overhead. Every so often, they would land on a tree or by a pond so Ori could rest. Mila would feed her breadcrumbs and told her how well she was doing. After landing in a glade, it was a surprise when Ori flew up into the air without them.

"Ah," Nathanial said watching her go. "Was she supposed to do that?"

Mila smirked. "This way," she said with a head gesture.

They went up to where a log sat against a rock.

"This is it," Mila said.

Nathanial could see the split of a Niche and for the first time he could see something more there. Outlined skyscrapers and the words *Credence Junction* seeped through like a water stain.

"You need to switch out of that Hyperion getup before we enter." Mila pointed to his casual T-shirt marked with the Hyperion logo.

After a week of changing clothes in front of each other in their P.E. class, Nathanial didn't think much of pulling off his T-shirt right there and slipping on his new blue-collared shimmer shirt. A few hops on one foot and then the other meant he soon had his multi-pocketed dancing pants on and was ready to go.

Mila smirked at his clothing again as she had when he'd bought the outfit and said, "You rival even my fashion taste for flair, Nat."

Nathanial eyed her muted tones of black and maroon, but thought her pound of necklaces might disagree with her comment. He shrugged and took it as a compliment.

Mila pressed her hand into the wood and pulled open the corner. They walked into the Niche.

It was always strange walking through a Niche, the way it's strange the first time you ride an elevator and the door opens to a whole new room, but this time it was absolutely jarring. He had stepped from a beautiful, bright, open glade into a bustling, claustrophobic, noisy, neon-light-blaring enclosure of a city that smelled like rotting fish.

"Whoa, what is this place?" Nathanial said with

a crinkled nose.

"Credence Junction," Mila said looking around. "About twenty Niches link here en route to other places. Makes for quite the cluster." She began elbowing her way through the crowd.

Nathanial was still gawking at all the glowing market stands when Mila took his arm and pulled him between the bumping bodies. They meandered through pedestrian alleys where food, clothes, bags, toys, and wing-muscle massages were continuously begging to be bought. The buildings around them were tall to the point of disappearing into the darkness beyond the jutting shops that catered solely to flying consumers. Not until after thwarting several skitzel-selling advances, did they finally come out of the hustle to a five-lane road.

Nathanial couldn't believe the sight of all the strange automobiles zipping by. How had sprites invented hovercrafts before humans? It just wasn't fair! He remembered the vehicle his attempted kidnapper had put him in. It seemed to be the popular choice of transportation here.

"Come on," Mila said pulling him down the sidewalk. "The Niche-way is just down here."

They stuck to the sidewalk along the busy street until they came to a tunnel. The hovercrafts were stopping and going through toll stations where payment was taken before they could continue. The sidewalk into the tunnel had a line of pedestrians waiting at a tollbooth of their own.

"We have to pay to go through here?" Nathanial asked, coming to the end of the line.

"Busy Niche-ways need upkeep," Mila said. "But more than coin, we need papers. I'm going to check if my contact had any luck, but he doesn't like strangers. Will you be ok saving our spot in line?"

Nathanial sighed and looked around. A group of men in boxy gray uniforms were patrolling the tollbooths. He had been chased by quite a few of those sprites the year before.

"Mila?" Nathanial said keeping an eye on the patrols.

"Yeah?"

"You don't think Hyperion would send an APB out on us, do you?"

"A what?"

Nathanial indicated the meaning of his worry with a head nod toward the uniformed officers.

Mila caught his meaning. "Maybe you should stick with me."

Nathanial turned to follow her, but ran smack into a tall sprite behind him.

"Excuse me," Nathanial mumbled looking straight at a pin on the man's shirt: diamond-encrusted keys crossing a sword. He fearfully looked up, sure he was going to find the dark-green kidnapper who had worn this symbol on a ring, glaring back down at him, but instead there was a pale face with inky streaks across the bridge of his nose.

Nathanial hurriedly moved to the side. The way his eyes kept watch of him sent a shiver down his spine.

Mila yanked Nathanial away from the eye-lock and lead him back into the crowd. "I shouldn't have brought you here," she was whispering in a panic. "I should have known you weren't just *any* human, but all I saw was that girl in your head. How could I have known it was you?"

Nathanial didn't like the fear in Mila's voice. What did she mean he wasn't just *any* human?

"What are you talking about?" Nathanial whispered frantically. "Did you see something in that sprite?"

"It's ok," she said more to herself than to him. "I know what to do."

They rushed down several stone stairways until the sound of the busy streets overhead became muffled. Mila approached a door in the large arched drain-way. She put her hand on the door and said, "Without the Skilla, there'd be no freedoms." The door opened.

Nathanial entered after Mila and the door closed behind them. They were in a sewage room with a small drainage river running across its center and into a large circular tunnel. Unless Nathanial had expected to find himself in the twisted lair of the Teenage Mutant Ninja Turtles, he wouldn't have expected this.

The brick walls were mostly covered in tapestries depicting a morbid sprite history, which put in humorous contrast the pink fuzzy rug lying beneath the small sitting area in the corner. Two red sectional couches formed a square around a trinket-covered coffee table and colorful Christmas lights illuminated the space overhead.

A sprite approached Mila from the handful of punk-attired purple youths that sat on the couches. With a large smile, he gave her a hug. He couldn't have been more than a couple of years older than Mila and he had similar skin tones to hers. The only difference was in the dark purple around his eyes. It spread wide across the top of his face. The rest of his skin was a lighter shade of purple and his contrasting dark hair stuck straight back on his head.

"Mila, I can't believe it's you! I heard you ran off to Hyperion," the sprite said through a straight-toothed grin. "Now, why would you want to go and change your stripes when the ones you were born to are so beautiful?"

"Yeah well, don't believe everything you hear," Mila smirked.

Nathanial was surprised by the lie. If this guy was like her, and he assumed he was, then couldn't he read minds, too? But they could probably block their own kind from that trick even better than others could, he thought.

"Anyway," Mila continued, "this is Nat. Nat, this is Zane."

Nathanial nodded and Zane gave a quick acknowledgment wave.

"We need to use your tunnel," Mila said holding her smile.

"Right to the point as always." Zane laughed. "Well, you know the price. Question is, are you actually going to pay it this time?"

"Now, Zane, what ever could you mean?" Mila said.

"I knew every time you used the tunnel, Mila. I just let you think you were that clever."

"Hmm..." Mila contemplated with a tight-lipped grin. "Well, in that case, if I were you, I'd up the price to make up the difference then."

Zane put his arm around Mila and began walking with her across the room. He said, "If you were me, you would, because that's what I would do, but if it was you in my position, then you wouldn't." He turned and put one hand on each of her shoulders, lowered his eyes to hers, and said, "and that's why I always let you get away with it." They hugged.

Nathanial felt uncomfortable with the flirty exchanges and turned his attention to the group on the couch. He found their complete attention was already on him, which only magnified his discomfort. He moved his gaze over the wall tapestries in hope that he looked truly fascinated by their history of struggle and woe, but the scenes of spears through guts and decapitations by the mound only put a deeper grimace upon his face.

There was a knock on the door directly behind Nathanial. One of the more decorated punk girls who adorned her mohawk with silver mouse skulls walked over from the couch to put her pierced browed eye to the peephole.

"It's a Swartza!" The girl frantically informed the group. "He followed the boy here. He suspects him of something." The girl narrowed her eyes at Nathanial. He recognized the look to be the same as Mila's just before she had unlocked all his memories. Her eyes were dilating.

Mila rushed forward and pulled Nathanial away.

"Why are you blocking me?" The girl screamed at Mila. "What are you hiding, and how could you lead a Swartza here? It's true what they say about you, isn't it? You've pulled away from your own kind!"

Mila pushed Nathanial farther behind her and stepped ferociously toward the accusing girl. "What I pull away from is ignorance preached as truth. Our blood abilities are not what make us kin. We will never mend the rifts torn before the treaty if we keep up like this. You might as well join the Swartza if you don't agree."

Everyone gasped as if Mila had slapped the girl.

"How dare you," she whispered fiercely and looked as though she might literally strike in return.

Zane stepped between them yelling, "We don't have time for this!" The girl looked intent on continuing her assault on Mila, but Zane stared her down until she backed off. He turned to Mila. "I don't know what you've gotten yourself into this time, Mila, but I wish you would remember the strife our kind has gone through for meddling in business that was not our own." He looked coldly to Nathanial.

"If the Skilla hadn't meddled then, none of us would have any of our freedoms," Mila retorted in a whisper.

Zane sighed. "Go through the tunnel. I'll make sure you aren't followed."

Mila looked worried at these words. Zane nodded and hugged her one last time.

Chapter Sixteen

THE DARK OFFER

*M*ila jumped down into the drainage stream that divided the Skilla's lair in two. The water splashed up just below her knees. The knocking on the door escalated to a beating. All of the remaining Skilla, except for Zane, crowded around its hostility.

"I don't know who you are or what you think you are doing," Zane said in an intense whisper to Nathanial, "but that girl you've dragged into your problems means the world to me, and if she gets hurt because of you…" Zane's eyes projected thoughts of punishment into Nathanial's mind; he had a clear picture of what he could expect if something were to happen to Mila.

Images of having his head dunked into a vat of lava were still burning on the back of his pupils when Nathanial squeaked out, "Got it!"

"Get out of here," Zane said, pushing Nathanial into the little river.

Nathanial ran into the water beside Mila, unable to shake Zane's implanted visions of brutality.

"Maybe you should stay behind," Nathanial said, gulping and rubbing his throat from a particularly creative image of him being strangled. *He* would never have thought to use intestines like that!

"What? No," Mila said stubbornly. She gripped Nathanial's arm and forced him through the tunnel behind her.

Nathanial knew right away what he had just stepped through. He had felt these sensations before—the feeling that every inch of him was being pulled and stretched as he traveled at deafening speeds. The last time he had gone through a tunnel like this was when he traveled from Thatcherville, the sprite settlement at his house, to the seaside town where the *Argosy* was docked; the pirate ship where he had met Aliya. He could see the white light at the end of the tunnel growing, and, although he felt like screaming and vomiting and hyperventilating all at the same time, there was an overwhelming ray of hope keeping everything inside of him together. Could he really be this close to Aliya already? Why hadn't Mila just taken them this way in the first place? It seemed the wait for the false ID had been pointless if this were the case.

Nathanial stumbled out of the darkness. Disappointment clouded his hope on sight of yet another patch of woods; it was not a sandy hillside, but it was confirmed that the tunnel was the same type as the one he had been in before. The trees were back to human perspective; he was no longer bug-sized. He could also assume they'd traveled a good distance.

"Where are we?" He asked Mila who was already up a small incline.

"Texas. There's a train station up here."

"Texas," Nathanial mumbled joining her. So that was probably why Mila had wanted to Niche-hop. He knew the *Argosy* was somewhere on the Atlantic coast. They still had a long way to go.

They were next to a road and on the other side was the train station. Nathanial did a double-take at Mila whose ears were rounded and all hints of her purple had vanished. She even had tones of pink in her complexion to complete her human appearance, though still a punk one, at that.

Nathanial quickly felt his own ear tips and panicked at their points. "Oh, no, I need to put my cuffs on before anyone sees me," he said reaching for the box in his rucksack.

Mila stopped him. "You don't need those," she tapped the concealed amulet under his shirt. "Concentrate on your ears and imagine gravity crushing the tips down. Push on them with your fingertips if it helps."

Nathanial looked at her uncertainly but slowly put his fingers on his ears and began to push them down. He didn't feel anything happening.

"I don't want to waste any more time," Nathanial said anxiously. He was finally going after Aliya. He was in Texas. He didn't want to stop to learn another stupid sprite trick when he had cuffs right there that could do it for him.

Mila snatched the cuffs out of his hand. "Don't be impatient. You're not a human anymore. You need to know this. Humans think everything is solid and unchanging, yet they grow and change constantly. Humans think things they can't see, can't be, but unseen energy still drives them. You are a sprite. You are tapped in. You can move the blocks that build you. You can harness the power that moves you. You can shrink your ear tips!"

Nathanial listened intently and felt pumped by the speech. She was right, even as a human he would get *feelings* about things: if someone was watching him, if someone didn't like him, if his mom was worrying, and even if a storm was coming. But he always dismissed these things as nothing; but maybe they weren't nothing. Maybe it was that humans ignored the tap because they couldn't *see* it. And maybe now that he was a sprite, not only could he see it running through the veins of a leaf and feel it in the heart of a squirrel, but he could manipulate it! The bending of the great tree, Hyperion, had proved as much. *Move the blocks that build you.*

And with that, his ear tips shrank.

"Thank you." Mila exaggeratedly exhaled. "Now we can go."

They went across the street toward a pink building and passed under a round stained-glass window that said *Sunset Station.*

Before Nathanial took another step, he spotted the men's restroom and said, "I'm going to go change out of these wet clothes," when what he really meant was no way would he be caught dead wearing this in the human world.

Mila said, "Yeah, I'm going, too. Meet you back at the ticket station over there."

Exiting his stall and feeling more like himself to be back in his old jeans and T-shirt, Nathanial washed his hands in the sink. He stared down at the water running from the faucet and recalled how the Hyperion faucets required a touch to pull the water out of the tree. Everything in the human world was connected with pipes and wires, whereas everything in the sprite world was...not. The world was already connected naturally and the sprites knew how to use that to their advantage.

Catching his reflection, Nathanial examined the person looking back at him. He still looked human, but he knew he wasn't. He'd been feeling that part of him slip away more and more each day. What would Aliya say to this? Would she trust him anymore? If there was a way to take it back, would he?

Boss had said he was stuck between two worlds. He couldn't be honest about who he was with the sprites, for fear of prejudice, and he couldn't let anyone from his human life know about his change, for fear they'd think him crazy. He hated not being able to tell his mom what he was experiencing. She was the queen of advice and comfort. How could he go the rest of his life without letting her in on it?

Nathanial sighed, shut off the faucet, dried his hands, and recovered his resolve to go find Aliya. He'd have to save the worries about the rest of his life for another time. For now, he hoped Aliya would understand that he did what he *had* to do to get them free of a factory's life and if she didn't like it, well, he would be up for any suggestions she had to fix it. The knowledge of the sprites that her Mataunte had passed on to her had helped them before; perhaps it could help them again.

Mila was already at an automated ticket-machine when Nathanial joined her. She pressed the *Routes* button as he peered over her shoulder.

"Looks like we can only go as far as New Orleans," he said, reading the touch screen. "It's seventy-one dollars each and it will take over fifteen hours!"

Mila put her hand on the screen. It flickered white and two tickets shot out from the slot below. "Let's go," she said.

Nathanial's mind reeled over the moral implications of what just happened and he was considering protesting when he froze at the strangest sight before him. Sprites at work were scattered throughout the station. One tickled a middle-aged woman's nose with a feather and caught the subsequent sneeze in a bag. Two flew around a toddler: one tripped him while the other bottled and corked his tears. A group of sprites were forming around a pet cage, but just seemed to be getting a kick out of making the little Pomeranian yap its tiny heart out.

Mila rushed over and whispered, "Stop staring. Do you want us to get noticed?"

Nathanial quickly looked away, but it was hard to pretend he couldn't see them.

Once onboard the stretching Amtrak train, they took the first two available blue-cushioned seats.

Nathanial did his best to ignore the sprites aboard their coughing, hacking, burping humans, and sat by the window on Mila's suggestion that it'd help him to put his attention elsewhere.

The train set off on its metal-rail fixed-course, and Nathanial's mind soon fell back onto the images of punishment Zane would initiate upon him if Mila suffered any injury. He contemplated bringing up the subject with her, but she looked quite focused on her tablet. Fifteen hours was a long time to sit in silence with such brutal thoughts, however, so he decided to make an attempt anyway.

"So is Zane, like, your boyfriend or something?" Nathanial ungracefully blurted out after all the different ways he'd internally recited the query.

Mila looked up at him, snorted, shook her head, and went back to her tablet.

"Was that a no?" Nathanial asked uncertainly. "He seems pretty fond of you."

Nathanial let the silence linger a moment in case she was pondering her response.

"It was kind of weird that you lied to him," he continued and received a fierce look. "What? I just mean, can't he read your mind? He's like you, right?"

"First of all, I don't exactly *read* minds," she rebuked. "Female Skilla receive sounds, voices, images—but then we must interpret them, and we don't always get it right. The males can send out those same sounds, voices, and images to others, but they choose what they send and it's up to the receivers to interpret the meanings."

"Ah…" Nathanial nodded and said, "that explains it."

"What?"

"Zane may have sent a little warning my way as to the sudden and brutal demise of my life if something were to happen to you."

Mila laughed. "Figures."

"Yeah, I'm thinking maybe you should go back to Hyperion. Now that I'm back in the human world, I'm pretty sure I can find my way from here."

"Don't be like that." Mila scoffed. "I can take care of myself. Nothing's going to happen to me that would send Zane after your pretty little head, so don't worry. And besides, I know about the *Argosy* and where it ports. The faery influence is still so strong there, it causes a continuous space/time warp. Sprites only go there to take the *Argosy* when they're in need of a *super* shortcut to Midtown. That place is on an island off the Bermuda Triangle, crazy-tricky to reach through conventional Niche hopping or airstreams or anything. Still, your sprites must have been desperate to have taken you on the *Argosy*; it's really dangerous, given you could get stuck in a time-loop aboard that thing, which you well know from what happened to Aliya. But you're trying to tell me you don't need me so, go ahead, tell me how to find the *Argosy*."

Nathanial grunted and said, "I thought I could just see it, now that I'm a sprite, and I have the battle blade for directions so..."

"Oh, yeah, I saw in your memories you were using it like a compass, right? How does it work? Does it point to your destiny or what?"

"I didn't think it was pointing to my destiny! I thought, more *Pirates of the Caribbean,* points to my heart's desire kind of thing."

"Hmm, your heart's desire and your destiny could be two separate things. Only if you're lucky are they the same. Didn't Bunny say something like, it points the way you are *supposed* to go? We'll have to test it out when the humans aren't around. Either way, I wouldn't rely on it to get you to the *Argosy*. Who knows where that thing points to. Just leave it to me."

Nathanial pondered all of this as he looked out the window, thinking back on when he'd used the battle blade to guide him to Midtown. Did it work because he'd wanted to get himself and Aliya to their wish sprites, or did it take him to his destiny of becoming a sprite? Bunny had made it sound like she knew it would lead him to Midtown. How could she have known if it was leading him to his destiny? Maybe she didn't know exactly how it worked either. Maybe everything up until that point had just been blind luck, yet the concept of destiny did not settle well with him. That would imply there was no control over his own life and that had been something he'd been fighting to gain ever since he'd learned of the sprites' control over him.

Deciding not to stress over the idea until he had a chance to test the battle blade, his mind found other things to worry about.

"What did you mean earlier, about I'm not just any human?" Nathanial asked.

Mila lifted a brow. "I saw a wanted poster of you in the mind of that Swartza in Credence Junction. I hadn't put it together until then. Everyone has heard of the human that ruined a headquarters town. You're infamous," Mila nodded. "That's the kind of thing that makes sprite headlines, if you know what I mean?"

Nathanial gulped, "Oh." He knew the word infamous meant famous in a bad way. The century kids probably would have literally rung his neck if they had found out that he was not only once a human but also an infamous one.

Mila was watching him. "I think they did know."

"What?" Nathanial snapped out of his head to listen.

"I think they did know who you were in the end. In fact, your diary confirmed it for them." She paused and knitted her fingers before proceeding. "There's been a rift growing in our culture for some time now. There's the forward-thinking progressive sprites who believe in equality and the right to choose the path of one's own life. Then there are the stagnant scum who were born into privilege and want the world the way that it was when they were at the top of the food chain. They don't want equal opportunities. That would put their position at risk. Those sprites have been fighting our progress quietly for decades, but I think they are about to get really loud."

"What does that have to do with the century kids knowing who I am?" Nathanial asked, trying to relate the two issues in his head.

"You represent the struggle, Nat. You are where the forward thinkers want to be headed. A human becoming a sprite—wow! That's way beyond what's been accepted up until now. Sprites like me are about as far as culture has been pushed to tolerate, and even *we* get the stink eye in many parts of the world."

"Because you want to change your blood traits?"

"Yes. Because we want something we weren't born to."

"And many sprites go to Hyperion to get that?"

Mila nodded.

"But why would sprites like Bron and his buddies be going to a school like that if they are so against the concept?"

"Oh, believe me, they don't want to be going to Hyperion," Mila said with a snort. "They'd much rather be at Swartza High. But that school is selective even amongst the century families. I'm sure their parents put them in Hyperion to cause trouble. They are always the ones starting petitions to halt classes they don't agree with. And, of course, it's good to know what the enemy is up to."

Nathanial gulped in understanding then asked, "So what do you want to be? Why did you choose Hyperion?"

Mila hesitated. Nathanial was expecting *none of your business* from that expression, but it quickly softened and she said, "I'd like to be a wish sprite."

Nathanial couldn't contain his grin. Imagining a punk rock wish sprite, it couldn't be helped.

"Oh, shut up, don't make me regret telling you!"

Mila said, sitting back heavily.

"I didn't say anything!" Nathanial defended in a laugh. "I think that's wonderful. I love wish sprites. My favorite kind of sprite, really."

Mila shook her head. "It's not that far off from what I am," she continued, avoiding eye contact. "My people are notorious for meddling in others' business—wish sprites do the same thing. I don't see why anyone should have a problem with it."

"I agree, they shouldn't. It's great. Really, Mila."

She still didn't look at him. She picked up her tablet and started swiping again, and mumbled, "It doesn't mean I'm not proud of my heritage or my people." Then she became very silent.

Across the aisle was a little boy sitting with his mother. The boy's head kept drooping forward. His mother put her arm around him and he fell over into her lap. She bundled her jacket into a pillow for him.

Nathanial hadn't realized how tired he was until then. The weight of all the running from Hyperion and the stress of Credence Junction piled onto him all at once. He pulled the gray hoodie Boss had given him out from his rucksack and made it into a pillow against the window. He stared out onto the rushing scenery of trees and flatlands until his eyelids drooped. He closed them, listening to the repetitive sounds of train on tracks, and let his worries fall into their hypnotic beat.

It wasn't an easy rest. In the darkness of his mind he called to Aliya. He could hear her crying out to him in return. She was close. He ran toward the sounds of her voice, but the faster he ran, the fainter her calls became. He stopped. From behind him, he could feel a presence. He turned and Aliya's captor, Cyron, was there, pushing his giant hand down upon Nathanial's face, holding him down. He punched and kicked with all of his strength, but couldn't move out from under the hold.

Nathanial woke and threw his rucksack onto the ground.

"Whoa, you ok?" Mila responded to Nathanial's fierce and panicked breathing.

Nathanial glared at Mila, unable to recognize her. Then awareness washed in. "Yeah," he finally said and shook off the anger. "How long was I out?"

"A good ten hours," Mila said munching on a piece of bread. "I had a little rest myself. You missed the food cart."

Nathanial groaned. His adrenaline faded quickly and he felt a grumble of hunger. He reached into his jeans pocket and was thankful to be correct in assuming he still had a couple of bucks tucked away. Looking up and down the dimly lit train he said, "I think there's a food car back there. I'm going to go check."

Mila stood and let Nathanial pass into the walkway. He wobbled through two train cars full of napping passengers before he entered the dining car. He only had enough money for a half of a turkey sandwich. He sat down on one of the stools that paired with a small table against the window and munched away as he stared out into the darkness.

The feeling of dread was growing within him. He couldn't take Cyron out on his own. The last time he'd faced him was proof of that. The nightmare had only been a reflection of the past. How was he going to get Aliya off the *Argosy* with that brute guarding her? He would have to do it without Cyron realizing he was there. He wished he had Bunny with him. She was good at making disguises.

"Hello Nathanial," a deep voice vibrated from the man who took the seat opposite him.

Nathanial's eyes widened. Though the look of the man had changed, his colorations were tan instead of green and he wore a business suit instead of a cloak, his voice was immediately recognizable. It was the voice that had offered to buy the magnifying glass for him at Hyperion and then proceeded to tell him he had no choice but to leave with him.

Nathanial stood up but the man grabbed his arm and said, "Wait. I'm here to make you an offer."

Nathanial looked down at the gripping hand, which proceeded to let go in a gesture of trust. Nathanial narrowed his eyes and sat back down. Without Boss around, his options were limited.

"I've been talking with my people and we realize it was rash to try and take you the way that I did back at Hyperion," the man said in uncharacteristic apology. "That's why I didn't make a second attempt and that's not what I'm here to do now. You are a sprite, one of us, and you should be treated with respect."

Nathanial frowned and said, "Versus the lack of respect a human deserves. Like when you shot me with an arrow, took my memories, and tried to revert me back to a factory."

The man shrugged and gave a crooked smile. Nathanial glowered and asked, "So what do you want?"

"Like I said, to make you an offer. The Swartza want to teach you. Hyperion is not a place where you can reach your full potential. They do things slowly and their techniques don't always work. We can guarantee your mastering all of your abilities. *And*," he held for dramatic effect, "we can get Aliya back for you."

"What?" Nathanial gasped. "But why would you do that? She's human…"

"We've been looking into her. She is more than she knows. We can teach you together."

Nathanial's heart sank. Aliya wouldn't want to be a sprite. She hated sprites! And he knew these were exactly the kind she had warned him about. He didn't know what these guys were up to, but knew they were involved in bad things, like kidnapping, for example.

Then again, what had Boss and Phlegm ever done for him but make him sick and try to repeal his wish to be well? Their goal had been to go back to work on him as *factory Nathanial* and now much of the time they seemed resentful they were stuck with *sprite Nathanial*! Maybe being jerks was just a sprite trait in general, and the Swartza would be no worse than his current guardians. Bunny and the wish sprites were the only ones who'd ever shown any kindness toward him, and they seemed to be overruled a lot.

"I don't know," Nathanial said. "Why do you want us? Aren't you kind of picky about who you let into your club?" He was thinking about how the century kids hadn't even been accepted by them.

"Yes," the man smiled, "and just the fact we offer you our hand in friendship says a lot about your fine character."

Nathanial didn't know what to do. An easy way to get Aliya back was right before him, but what would the repercussions be? What would he be dragging her into as a result?Phlegm had said the Swartza were like a cult. He pictured people in dark cloaks chanting around a star of candles and making goat sacrifices when he heard that word, but surely that couldn't be right, could it?

He needed some advice and he felt completely alone until he heard, "Why don't you go back to the scum of the slugs where you came from, you slimy Swartza! Nat's not interested!" It was Mila and she was furious. She pulled Nathanial off his stool and stepped in front of him.

The Swartza stood up, glaring at Mila. "Let the boy decide for himself," he growled.

"You know good and well that Nat has no idea what your kind has done and what you are still capable of doing if you aren't stopped, but, believe me, I'll be sure to fill him in, and he'll never join you!"

"Everything we've done is for the betterment of sprite-kind. All your liberties and luxuries you hold dear came from the accomplishments of the Swartza you spit on."

"Don't try to feed me your political rhetoric! I am a Skilla! I know what is true!"

The man shook his head, "If you are Skilla, then there is no reasoning with you. Your kind is blinded by hate." He then looked to Nathanial. "Do not always listen to those closest to you just because they are close, Nathanial. Look for the answers yourself before you deny the correct path. If you want to find me, just call a raven and it'll bring you to me."

"Don't listen to him, Nat!" Mila said pushing Nathanial back but there was nothing more to listen to. The man had gone.

Nathanial looked to the food bar attendant to see if her mind had just been blown by the vanishing of a man, but surprisingly her eyes were averted and uninterested. Mila pushed Nathanial out of the train car until he picked up his own speed.

"I can't believe the nerve of him," Mila said as they plunked back down into their blue seats. "You weren't considering his offer, were you?"

Nathanial pondered. This was obviously an insulting response. Mila hit him on the shoulder saying, "Don't even think about it! The Swartza are at the heart of the inequality I told you about. They cripple sprite progress and follow no moral code to reach their ends. They speak of the betterment of sprites, but they do horrible things at the cost to others to accomplish it. You know firsthand that's true. Their political victories are why factories are no longer protected from overuse. They are why you were allowed to be kept sick and would still be sick if it weren't for the wish sprites' interference. Keeping a boy permanently sick for profit is the kind of thing they do for sprite betterment, and that's not even the worst of it."

"Ok, so the Swartza are bad, I get it," Nathanial said. "But you have to remember who actually kept me sick. That was headquarters, *sprite* headquarters, and the two sprites that were working on me are now my mentors at Hyperion. I'm not sure they are much better than that dude back there."

Mila brushed her ringed fingers through her dark hair in frustration and persisted, "I know it's confusing from your perspective, but I'm telling you that headquarters only has authority to keep kids sick because of the work the Swartza do," Mila said in dramatic explanation.

"You know," Nathanial said, just about fed up, "I really don't care. I just became a sprite to get Aliya off that ship. I don't want to stay one. I don't really like sprites. You're all a bunch of selfish jerks!"

Nathanial felt empowered by the statement. He'd been struggling with that decision and this last encounter had decided it for him. He didn't want to get involved in all these twisted sprite politics. If he could rescue Aliya with the power of being a sprite, then that would have made it worth it, but after that, there would be no reason to make himself live as one. There was too much hostility toward him in the sprite world and he wanted to get back home to where he was loved.

Mila glared at Nathanial. "Oh, do you think we're the only selfish jerks? I could tell you some stories about some selfish jerks; about those who thought themselves so much better than the rest that they began the first rebellion to seek out and conquer the world. Who grew to forget they were kin as they grew in height, and drenched the globe in their own people's blood to establish dominance...who tried to take advantage of their sprite cousins and only offered abuse in return. Oh, I could tell you some stories, changeling."

Nathanial sighed and shook his head. She was talking about humans. Aliya had told him the story of how sprites and humans used to live symbiotically until humans began taking advantage. Of course humans were as flawed as sprites, and, if they really did all originate from the same place, then it made sense.

"Ok, I'm sorry," he finally said. "I realize humans and sprites have a twisted history with faults on both sides. I shouldn't judge sprites when humans have done horrible things, too. I just don't want to get involved in this conflict. It was a desperate decision to become a sprite and I'm afraid it was the wrong move. I was just getting a normal life back home. If I can free Aliya, and we can remove her curse, then that will be that. I should go home."

Mila's contemplation held Nathanial's until she said, "You may not want to take the path before you right now because, yeah, it's scary standing up for something you know to be wrong when the rest of the world is telling you it's not. But you chose this path. You may have done it for you and your friend, but now it's bigger than the two of you. If all that I have seen in you is true, and I hope that it is, then you won't be running back home anytime soon."

Chapter Seventeen

THE FINAL CAW

$\mathcal{M}$ila was skimming her tablet and scrolling through a plane of intersecting lines. Nathanial assumed she would eventually tell him what she was up to, but after a half an hour of silence, his curiosity was bursting.

"Finally," she blurted out giving Nathanial an excited jump. "We're approaching a low-flowing airstream."

Mila stood up, grabbed her bag, and slung it over her shoulder, but kept her tablet in hand.

"What?" Nathanial asked uncertain if he should follow.

"It's obvious the Swartza has a track on you," Mila said intensely. "They probably did it with the same arrow that took your memories. I had us on this human transport to keep you hidden after we had to ditch the quicker route of Niche-hopping, but even a false ID wouldn't have protected us from that Swartza finding you. It's just about getting you to Aliya as fast as we can now—and to do that, we need to catch the next airstream." She started walking down the aisle. When Nathanial didn't follow, she added, "Well, come on!"

Nathanial complied and they entered a space that connected two passenger cars. Mila approached the door leading to the outside and began the attempt to pry it open.

"What are you doing? I'm not jumping from a moving train!" Nathanial shouted over the rumbling beat of iron wheels against the tracks.

"Help me out here, would ya," Mila said ignoring the protest.

Nathanial hesitated. Mila gave him a commanding stare. He went to help and together they opened the door.

"We need to get to the roof," Mila shouted from the edge of the howling darkness.

Nathanial shook his head.

"You asked me to come on this trip to guide you, remember? You're going to have to trust me if you want Aliya back."

Mila swung out of the train car and onto a bolted metal ladder.

Nathanial knelt down with his rucksack and pulled out his geck-gloves. "I can't believe I'm doing this," he mumbled to himself and slid on the confidence boosters. He secured his rucksack to his back and then bravely reached out for the exterior ladder.

It was cold and windy on the top of the train. That made it difficult for Nathanial to hear Mila. She was looking at her tablet and shouting, "It's coming up just around this bend."

She put the tablet into her rucksack and clipped its straps snug around her waist. "You still have that dust?"

It took Nathanial a moment to comprehend, as he was preoccupied with a vision of himself falling from the speeding train, but then he pulled the dust from his rucksack.

"Right," Mila said, "give me a handful."

Nathanial poured the sparkling sand carefully into her cupped hand and then scooped a fistful for himself. He didn't like where this was headed.

"When I say so, throw the dust into the air and jump through it."

Nathanial was still shaking his head in disbelief.

Mila laughed. "It's going to be fine. I do this sort of thing all the time!"

Mila looked ahead of her and saw they were coming around the bend. "Ok, on the count of three, you ready?"

Nathanial was not going to stop shaking his head no.

"You better do it or you'll be left behind," Mila

warned. "One…two…three!"

He did it. It was unbelievable, but he did it. Nathanial jumped up through the dust to pop back to bug-size. His flailing limbs were swept up into a windy gust. He was twisting and turning for a few delirious moments before he spread out his arms and legs to get a grip on the force around him, and thankfully stopped tumbling. With his head no longer spinning, he could see Mila just ahead of him. She was watching him from her Superman pose and gave him the thumbs-up.

The airstream that they had caught soon veered away from the train which continued around the bend and into the distance. The night's scenery zipped by in a blur until the dark blues gave way to streaming golden rays that signaled sunrise.

Nathanial's comfort level kicked up a few notches after some time in the airstream. Once a longer while had passed, he was surprised at boredom's nerve for settling in. He decided to fiddle around with maneuvering. Lifting up was simple enough; he could just arch his back. Dipping down proved to be trickier. He lowered his head and lifted his legs, which sent him rolling over himself. He didn't feel much like trying that one again. Side to side by a simple tilt of the body was the better bet.

Mila watched him amusedly for a while,

and then slowed herself down to fly beside him. "Having fun?" She asked.

"Yeah," Nathanial said confidently.

"We're almost there."

Nathanial's eyes widened, "As in…"

"Yeah," Mila said beaming "Look." She pointed out of the airstream to her right.

With the sun glinting solid over the ocean, and a light sparkling upon its waves, it became easier to see beyond the airstream and out onto a mirage-like vision of a sixteenth-century seaside town. It had cobbled streets and earthy buildings, and four massive ships docked at wooden piers.

"We can exit here," Mila said holding out her hand to Nathanial. He took it and they popped out the side of the airstream.

It was a bit of a fall, but as they had been traveling only a couple of bus lengths high over the plains, their featherweight bodies only needed the springy bend and rough texture of the tall grass blade they hit to slow them the rest of their sliding descent down.

"Guess we should go ahead and use the dust to get big again," Nathanial said reaching for it. A groan accompanied his sight upon its retrieval. "Getting low, but there's enough for now and maybe once more if we're lucky."

With a dusty dry splash, they were back to tromping human size and made their way along the upper beachside, over the sand and through the tall golden grass. The closer they came to the town's entrance, the more excited and anxious Nathanial became.

"Hold on a sec," Mila said before they were too close. "Why don't you try your battle blade compass trick? We can test that destiny-versus-heart's-desire theory."

"Oh, yes! Good idea!" Nathanial licked his lips and pulled the blade from his ankle. He held the point down over his palm and dropped it. Mila gasped.

"*Brujula*," Nathanial commanded, and they watched the blade spin before lying down in his palm.

"Hmm, it's pointing away from the *Argosy*," Mila said contemplatively.

"Yeah," Nathanial groaned putting the blade back into its holster. "So maybe it does point to destiny because I definitely *want* to go toward the *Argosy*. Either way, I'm not turning back now."

Walking into the small port town felt like he was stepping through a veil into the past, and Nathanial guessed he had done just that. People were dressed in handmade clothes sewn from cotton or wool, with jackets made from cowhide and shoes of leather or straw. The people walked from shop to shop, buying or selling, as if this was the way it'd always been and always should be.

Nathanial found himself slowing with an uneasy feeling washing over him. He heard several caws and turned his head to see a raven on a post back where they'd entered the town. It was unsettling, but he ignored it and continued deeper into town. He wasn't going to let anything distract him now.

They'd almost reached the *Argosy* when the sight of three figures stopped them in their tracks.

"Nooo…" Nathanial moaned.

Mila squinted at the figures and asked, "Is that Mr. P?"

It wasn't just Mr. P, but Boss and Bunny as well. The three were walking toward them, their skin tones no longer colorful shades and their human clothes in fashion with the surrounding century.

Nathanial thought about running for the *Argosy*, but stood stiffly in place. When Boss halted in front of him, Nathanial said, "You can't stop me from getting Aliya off that ship."

Boss looked at him, sad and disappointed.

Mila cleared her throat. "How'd you guys find us?"

Mr. P licked his upper teeth and said, "Bunny

can find anything that's used her dust in the last twenty-four hours."

"Oh, yeah," Mila nodded as if remembering the truth of that fact. She turned to Bunny. "That's you, then? You gave Nat the dust?"

Bunny nodded saying, "Sure did! Never know when you're gonna need the stuff!"

Boss and Nathanial continued staring each other down until Boss said, "We wouldn't have needed Bunny's dust-track to know where you were going."

Nathanial lifted his eyebrows. "Of course not. You knew I wanted to go after her and that's why you wouldn't tell me the truth about her when I asked."

"Exactly! That's exactly why I didn't tell you." Boss said, his temper on the rise. "Did you forget about her blood curse or about Cyron? Do you think he'd ever let you get close to her again? You're just a kid with no idea how to use your abilities. What do you expect to do? Just walk up there and take her? Do you remember what happened last time you tried to take her from him? He pushed you down like a wet doll."

"Well, I sure as hell don't plan on sitting back and doing nothing the way you clearly are!" Nathanial shouted.

"Boys, boys," Mila said putting her hands up. "I didn't come all this way without a plan. Cyron doesn't know who I am. I can get on that boat without a hitch. Aliya is as good as saved!"

Boss looked over to Mila's confident expression and squashed it by saying, "Well, sure, that'd be fine then, except Aliya isn't on the *Argosy* anymore."

"What?" Nathanial's heart plummeted.

"Cyron pulled her off this morning when the ship reappeared at sunrise," Boss said and looked back at Nathanial. "They must have known you were coming."

"And you just let him do that?" Nathanial yelled.

"Why do you always expect the worst of me?" Boss questioned seriously. "Don't you think I've tried to get Aliya back? I represented her at her hearing. I fought for her as I fought for you all year. When Bunny told me you were coming this way, I tried to head you off and negotiate a final time with Cyron, but it was too late. They were already gone, Nathanial."

Nathanial didn't know what to say. He'd thought Boss had only come there to drag him kicking and screaming back to Hyperion to resume the obligated mentorship. He didn't think Boss cared about Aliya and didn't want his running after her to complicate his life. But if what Boss was saying was true, then maybe he did care.

"So what do we do now?" Nathanial asked hopefully.

"Nathanial," Boss's tone dropped sorrowfully, "there's nothing we can do now. These things take time. We'll have to file an inquiry."

"What?"

"Phlegm is taking you back to Hyperion," Boss continued. "Bunny and I will go to new headquarters."

"No," Nathanial said with reddening eyes. "It's your headquarters that benefits from her being a factory— your headquarters that keeps kids trapped for profit."

"Nathanial," Boss said putting his hands out toward him.

"No," Nathanial slapped his hands away. "You lost her at her hearing last year, and you almost lost me this year! If I hadn't sprouted my ears at my birthday party, I would have been reverted back to a factory! I can't trust you to save her, Boss! I have to get her back myself!"

Without another word, riding on impulse, Nathanial turned and ran.

"What does he think he's doing?" Boss said shaking his head.

"Nothing good," Mila said worriedly and started

running after Nathanial.

Nathanial gathered the remaining dust in his palm, threw the empty bag aside, and shouted, "Raven!" The black bird flew off its perch and glided toward Nathanial.

"Nat, stop! Think about what you're doing!" Mila was screaming as she ran after him. "This isn't the way! I'll help you!"

But Nathanial wouldn't listen. He had been given a sure way to get Aliya back, and this was his opportunity to take it. There was no time to waste. They'd both wasted enough time under the control of sprites.

Nathanial tossed the dust into the air before him and jumped. The raven swooped low and Nathanial took hold of its feathery back. They were in the air and soaring away from the *Argosy*.

Bunny, Boss, and Phlegm caught up to Mila who was panting on the beach.

"Bunny," Phlegm gasped, "can you track 'em?"

Bunny shook her head sorrowfully. "Not as long as he's with that raven."

"That's exactly why the Swartza sent one," Boss said, grimacing.

"I can't believe he did it," Mila said hoarsely. "I can't believe it."

"What's going on, Mila?" Phlegm asked.

"What's he doing?"

"He has no idea," Mila said looking over to Phlegm and shaking her head. "No idea at all."

But Nathanial wouldn't have agreed if he had heard those words. He knew exactly what he was doing, what he had to do. He wasn't letting anyone stop him anymore. There was no more waiting.

Boss didn't think Nathanial could face Cyron, but he was wrong. He could do it for her. Mila thought he shouldn't deal with the Swartza, but *he* was the one with the plan now, not her. Her way had failed. It was time to take control.

Aliya knew everything about sprites and he was a sprite. He would free her and they would figure out what to do together, just like they had before.

Nathanial asked his battle blade one last time which way to go. It pointed in the direction the raven was flying. He put the dagger away with a new and confident resolve.

"I'm coming, Aliya," he whispered, and gripped tight to the black feathers of fortune that urged him on toward his destiny.

TO BE CONTINUED IN BOOK 3

NATHANIAL THATCHER
THE DIAMOND TRIALS